GEORGIA SLAVE NARRATIVES

A Folk History of Slavery in Georgia from Interviews with Former Slaves

* * *

Typewritten records prepared by
THE FEDERAL WRITERS' PROJECT
1936-1938

* * *

Published in cooperation with
THE LIBRARY OF CONGRESS

APPLEWOOD BOOKS
Bedford, Massachusetts

The LIBRARY
of CONGRESS

A portion of the proceeds from the sale of this book is donated to the Library of Congress, which holds the original Slave Narratives in its collection.

Thank you for purchasing an Applewood book. Applewood reprints America's lively classics --books from the past that are still of interest to modern readers. For a free copy of our current catalog, write to:

Applewood Books
P.O. Box 365
Bedford, MA 01730

ISBN 1-55709-013-0

FOREWORD

More than 140 years have elapsed since the ratification of the Thirteenth Amendment to the U.S. Constitution declared slavery illegal in the United States, yet America is still wrestling with the legacy of slavery. One way to examine and understand the legacy of the 19th Century's "peculiar institution" in the 21st century is to read and listen to the stories of those who actually lived as slaves. It is through a close reading of these personal narratives that Americans can widen their understanding of the past, thus enriching the common memory we share.

The American Folklife Center at the Library of Congress is fortunate to hold a powerful and priceless sampling of sound recordings, manuscript interviews, and photographs of former slaves. The recordings of former slaves were made in the 1930s and early 1940s by folklorists John A. and Ruby T. Lomax, Alan Lomax, Zora Neale Hurston, Mary Elizabeth Barnicle, John Henry Faulk, Roscoe Lews, and others. These aural accounts provide the only existing sound of voices from the institution of slavery by individuals who had been held in bondage three generations earlier. These voices can be heard by visiting the web site http://memory.loc.gov/ammem/collections/voices/. Added to the Folklife Center collections, many of the narratives from manuscript sources, which you find in this volume, were collected under the auspices of the United States Works Progress Administration (WPA), and were known as the slave narrative collection. These transcripts are found in the Library of Congress Manuscript Division. Finally, in addition to the Folklife Center photographs, a treasure trove of Farm Security Administration (FSA) photographs (including those of many former slaves) reside in the Prints and Photographs Division here at the nation's library. Together, these primary source materials on audio tape, manuscript and photographic formats are a unique research collection for all who would wish to study and understand the emotions, nightmares, dreams, and determination of former slaves in the United States.

The slave narrative sound recordings, manuscript materials, and photographs are invaluable as windows through which we can observe and be touched by the experiences of slaves who lived in the mid-19th century. At the same time, these archival materials are the fruits of an extraordinary documentary effort of the 1930s. The federal government, as part of its response to the Great Depression, organized unprecedented national initiatives to document the lives, experiences, and cultural traditions of ordinary Americans. The slave narratives, as documents of the Federal Writers Project, established and delineated our modern concept of "oral history." Oral history, made possible by the advent of sound recording technology, was "invented" by folklorists, writers, and other cultural documentarians under the aegis of the Library of Congress and various WPA offices—especially the Federal Writers' project—during the 1930s. Oral history has subsequently become both a new tool for the discipline of history, and a new cultural pastime undertaken in homes, schools, and communities by Americans of all walks of life. The slave narratives you read in the pages that follow stand as our first national exploration of the idea of oral history, and the first time that ordinary Americans were made part of the historical record.

The American Folklife Center has expanded upon the WPA tradition by continuing to collect oral histories from ordinary Americans. Contemporary projects such as our Veterans History Project, StoryCorps Project, Voices of Civil Rights Project, as well as our work to capture the stories of Americans after September 11, 2001 and of the survivors of Hurricanes Katrina and Rita, are all adding to the Library of Congress holdings that will enrich the history books of the future. They are the oral histories of the 21st century.

Frederick Douglas once asked: can "the white and colored people of this country be blended into a common nationality, and enjoy together...under the same flag, the inestimable blessings of life, liberty, and the pursuit of happiness, as neighborly citizens of a common country? I believe they can." We hope that the words of the former slaves in these editions from Applewood Books will help Americans achieve Frederick Douglas's vision of America by enlarging our understanding of the legacy of slavery in all of our lives. At the same time, we in the American Folklife Center and the Library of Congress hope these books will help readers understand the importance of oral history in documenting American life and culture—giving a voice to all as we create our common history.

Peggy Bulger
Director, The American Folklife Center
Library of Congress

A NOTE FROM THE PUBLISHER

Since 1976, Applewood Books has been republishing books from America's past. Our mission is to build a picture of America through its primary sources. The book you hold in your hand is a testament to that mission. Published in cooperation with the Library of Congress, this collection of slave narratives is reproduced exactly as writers in the Works Progress Administration's Federal Writers' Project (1936–1938) originally typed them.

As publishers, we thought about how to present these documents. Rather than making them more readable by resetting the type, we felt that there was more value in presenting the narratives in their original form. We believe that to fully understand any primary source, one must understand the period of time in which the source was written or recorded. Collected seventy years after the emancipation of American slaves, these narratives had been preserved by the Library of Congress, fortunately, as they were originally created. In 1941, the Library of Congress microfilmed the typewritten pages on which the narratives were originally recorded. In 2001, the Library of Congress digitized the microfilm and made the narratives available on their American Memory web site. From these pages we have reproduced the original documents, including both the marks of the writers of the time and the inconsistencies of the type. Some pages were missing or completely illegible, and we have used a simple typescript provided by the Library of Congress so that the page can be read. Although the font occasionally can make these narratives difficult to read, we believe that it is important not only to preserve the narratives of the slaves but also to preserve the documents themselves, thereby commemorating the groundbreaking effort that produced them. That way, also, we can give you, the reader, not only a collection of the life stories of ex-slaves, but also a glimpse into the time in which these stories were collected, the 1930s.

These are powerful stories by those who lived through slavery. No institution was more divisive in American history than slavery. From the very founding of America and to the present day, slavery has touched us all. We hope these real stories of real lives are preserved for generations of Americans to come.

Please note: This volume is not the complete collection of narratives that were recorded for this state. The additional parts are available in additional volumes from Applewood Books. For the purposes of listing the narratives included in this book, we have provided the original typewritten contents page and placed a box around the narratives included in this volume.

INFORMANTS

PLANTATION LIFE

RACHEL ADAMS
300 ODD STREET
ATHENS, GEORGIA

Written by: Sadie B. Hornsby (White)
Athens -

Edited by: Sarah H. Hall
Athens -

and

John N. Booth
District Supervisor
Federal Writers' Project
Residencies 6 & 7.
Augusta, Georgia.

RACHEL ADAMS
Ex-Slave - Age 78.

Rachel Adams' two-room, frame house is perched on the side of a steep hill where peach trees and bamboo form dense shade. Stalks of corn at the rear of the dwelling reach almost to the roof ridge and a portion of the front yard is enclosed for a chicken yard. Stepping gingerly around the amazing number of nondescript articles scattered about the small veranda, the visitor rapped several times on the front door, but received no response. A neighbor said the old woman might be found at her son's store, but she was finally located at the home of a daughter.

Rachel came to the front door with a sandwich of hoecake and cheese in one hand and a glass of water in the other. "Dis here's Rachel Adams," she declared. "Have a seat on de porch." Rachel is tall, thin, very black, and wears glasses. Her faded pink outing wrapper was partly covered by an apron made of a heavy meal sack. Tennis shoes, worn without hose, and a man's black hat completed her outfit.

Rachel began her story by saying: "Miss, dats been sich a long time back dat I has most forgot how things went. Anyhow I was borned in Putman County 'bout two miles from Eatonton, Georgia. My Ma and Pa was 'Melia and Isaac Little and, far as I knows, dey was borned and bred in dat same county. Pa, he was sold away from Ma when I was still a baby. Ma's job was to weave all de cloth for de white folks. I have wore many a dress made out of de homespun what she wove. Dere was 17 of us chillun, and I can't 'member de names of but two of 'em now - dey was John and Sarah. John was Ma's onliest son; all de rest of de other 16 of us was gals.

"Us lived in mud-daubed log cabins what had old stack chimblies made out of sticks and mud. Our old home-made beds didn't have no slats or metal springs neither. Dey used stout cords for springs. De cloth what dey made the ticks of dem old hay mattresses and pillows out of was so coarse dat it scratched us little chillun most to death, it seemed lak to us dem days. I kin still feel dem old hay mattresses under me now. Evvy time I moved at night it sounded lak de wind blowin' through dem peach trees and bamboos 'round de front of de house whar I lives now.

"Grandma Anna was 115 years old when she died. She had done wore herself out in slavery time. Grandpa, he was sold off somewhar. Both of 'em was field hands.

"Potlicker and cornbread was fed to us chillun, out of big old wooden bowls. Two or three chillun et out of de same bowl. Grown folks had meat, greens, syrup, cornbread, 'taters and de lak. 'Possums! I should say so. Dey cotch plenty of 'em and atter dey was kilt Ma would scald 'em and rub 'em in hot ashes and dat clean't 'em jus' as pretty and white. OO-o-o but dey was good. Lord, Yessum! Dey used to go fishin' and rabbit huntin' too. Us jus' fotched in game galore den, for it was de style dem days. Dere warn't no market meat in slavery days. Seemed lak to me in dem days dat ash-roasted 'taters and groundpeas was de best somepin t'eat what anybody could want. 'Course dey had a gyarden, and it had somepin of jus' about evvything what us knowed anything 'bout in de way of gyarden sass growin' in it. All de cookin' was done in dem big old open fireplaces what was fixed up special for de pots and ovens. Ashcake was most as good as 'taters cooked in de ashes, but not quite.

"Summertime, us jus' wore homespun dresses made lak de slips dey use for underwear now. De coats what us wore over our wool dresses in winter was knowed as 'sacques' den, 'cause dey was so loose fittin'. Dey was heavy and had wool in 'em too. Marse Lewis, he had a plenty of sheep, 'cause dey was bound to have lots of warm winter clothes, and den too, dey lakked mutton to eat. Oh! dem old brogan shoes was coarse and rough. When Marse Lewis had a cow kilt dey put de hide in de tannin' vat. When de hides was ready, Uncle Ben made up de shoes, and sometimes dey let Uncle Jasper holp him if dere was many to be made all at one time. Us wore de same sort of clothes on Sunday as evvyday, only dey had to be clean and fresh when dey was put on Sunday mornin'.

"Marse Lewis Little and his wife, Miss Sallie, owned us, and Old Miss, she died long 'fore de surrender. Marse Lewis, he was right good to all his slaves; but dat overseer, he would beat us down in a minute if us didn't do to suit him. When dey give slaves tasks to do and dey warn't done in a certain time, dat old overseer would whup 'em 'bout dat. Marster never had to take none of his Niggers to court or put 'em in jails neither; him and de overseer sot 'em right. Long as Miss Sallie lived de carriage driver driv her and Marse Lewis around lots, but atter she died dere warn't so much use of de carriage. He jus' driv for Marse Lewis and piddled 'round de yard den.

"Some slaves larnt to read and write. If dey went to meetin' dey had to go wid deir white folks 'cause dey didn't have no sep'rate churches for de Niggers 'til atter de war. On our Marster's place, slaves didn't go off to meetin' a t'all. Dey jus' went 'round to one another's houses and sung songs. Some of 'em read de Bible by heart. Once I heared a man preach what didn't know how to read one word in de Bible, and he didn't even have no Bible yit.

"De fust baptizin' I ever seed was atter I was nigh 'bout grown. If a slave from our place ever jined up wid a church 'fore de war was over, I never heared tell nothin' 'bout it.

"Lordy, Miss! I didn't know nothin' 'bout what a funeral was dem days. If a Nigger died dis mornin', dey sho' didn't waste no time a-puttin' him right on down in de ground dat same day. Dem coffins never had no shape to 'em; dey was jus' squar-edged pine boxes. Now warn't dat turrible?

"Slaves never went nowhar widout dem patterollers beatin' 'em up if dey didn't have no pass.

"Dere was hunderds of acres in dat dere plantation. Marse Lewis had a heap of slaves. De overseer, he had a bugle what he blowed to wake up de slaves. He blowed it long 'fore day so dat dey could eat breakfast and be out dere in de fields waitin' for de sun to rise so dey could see how to wuk, and dey stayed out dar and wukked 'til black dark. When a rainy spell come and de grass got to growin' fast, dey wukked dem slaves at night, even when de moon warn't shinin'. On dem dark nights one set of slaves helt lanterns for de others to see how to chop de weeds out of de cotton and corn. Wuk was sho' tight dem days. Evvy slave had a task to do atter dey got back to dem cabins at night. Dey each one had to spin deir stint same as de 'omans, evvy night.

"Young and old washed deir clothes Sadday nights. Dey hardly knowed what Sunday was. Dey didn't have but one day in de Christmas, and de only diff'unce dey seed dat day was dat dey give 'em some biscuits on Christmas day. New Year's Day was rail-splittin' day. Dey was told how many rails was to be cut, and dem Niggers better split dat many or somebody was gwine to git beat up.

"I don't 'member much 'bout what us played, 'cept de way us run 'round in a ring. Us chillun was allus skeered to play in de thicket nigh de house 'cause Raw Head and Bloody Bones lived dar. Dey used to skeer us out 'bout red 'taters. Dey was fine 'taters, red on de outside and pretty and white on de inside, but white folks called 'em 'nigger-killers.' Dat was one of deir tricks to keep us from stealin' dem 'taters. Dere warn't nothin' wrong wid dem 'taters; dey was jus' as good and healthy as any other 'taters.

Aunt Lucy, she was de cook, and she told me dat slaves was skeered of dem 'nigger-killer' 'taters and never bothered 'em much den lak dey does de yam patches dese days. I used to think I seed ha'nts at night, but it allus turned out to be somebody dat was tryin' to skeer me.

"'Bout de most fun slaves had was at dem corn-shuckin's. De general would git high on top of de corn pile and whoop and holler down leadin' dat cornshuckin' song 'til all de corn was done shucked. Den come de big eats, de likker, and de dancin'. Cotton pickin's was big fun too, and when dey got through pickin' de cotton dey et and drunk and danced 'til dey couldn't dance no more.

"Miss, white folks jus' had to be good to sick slaves, 'cause slaves was property. For Old Marster to lose a slave, was losin' money. Dere warn't so many doctors dem days and home-made medicines was all de go. Oil and turpentine, camphor, assfiddy (asafetida), cherry bark, sweetgum bark; all dem things was used to make teas for grown folks to take for deir ailments. Red oak bark tea was give to chillun for stomach mis'ries.

"All I can ricollect 'bout de comin' of freedom was Old Marster tellin' us dat us was free as jack-rabbits and dat from den on Niggers would have to git deir own somepin t'eat. It warn't long atter dat when dem yankees, wid pretty blue clothes on come through our place and dey stole most evvything our Marster had.

Dey kilt his chickens, hogs, and cows and tuk his hosses off and sold 'em. Dat didn't look right, did it?

"My aunt give us a big weddin' feast when I married Tom Adams, and she sho' did pile up dat table wid heaps of good eatments. My weddin' dress was blue, trimmed in white. Us had six chillun, nine grandchillun, and 19 great-grandchillun. One of my grandchillun is done been blind since he was three weeks old. I sont him off to de blind school and now he kin git around 'most as good as I kin. He has made his home wid me ever since his Mammy died.

"'Cordin' to my way of thinkin', Abraham Lincoln done a good thing when he sot us free. Jeff Davis, he was all right too, 'cause if him and Lincoln hadn't got to fightin' us would have been slaves to dis very day. It's mighty good to do jus' as you please, and bread and water is heaps better dan dat somepin t'eat us had to slave for.

"I jined up wid de church 'cause I wanted to go to Heben when I dies, and if folks lives right dey sho' is gwine to have a good restin' place in de next world. Yes Mam, I sho b'lieves in 'ligion, dat I does. Now, Miss, if you ain't got nothin' else to ax me, I'se gwine home and give dat blind boy his somepin t'eat."

....

Dist. 6. Ex Slv. #4. 9

MAY 8 1937

Washington Allen, Ex-Slave.

Born: December ______, 1854.

Place of birth: "Some where" in South Carolina.

Present Residence: 1932 ____ Fifth Avenue, Columbus, Georgia.

Interviewed: December 18, 1936.

The story of "Uncle Wash", as he is familiarly known, is condensed as follows:

He was born on the plantation of a Mr. Washington Allen of South Carolina, for whom he was named. This Mr. Allen had several sons and daughters, and of these, one son - Mr. George Allen - who, during the 1850's left his South Carolina home and settled near LaFayette, Alabama. About 1858, Mr. Washington Allen died and the next year, when "Wash" was "a five - year old shaver", the Allen estate in South Carolina was divided - - all except the Allen Negro slaves. These, at the instance and insistence of Mr. George Allen, were taken to LaFayette, Alabama, to be sold. All were put on the block and auctioned off, Mr. George Allen buying every Negro, so that not a single slave family was divided up.

"Uncle Wash" does not remember what he "fetched at de sale", but he does distinctly remember that as he stepped up on the block to be sold, the auctioneer ran his hand "over my head and said:

Genilmens, dis boy is as fine as split silk". Then, when Mr. George Allen had bought all the Allen slaves, it dawned upon them, and they appreciated, why he had insisted on their being sold in Alabama, rather than in South Carolina.

Before he was six years of age, little "Wash" lost his mother and, from then until freedom, he was personally cared for and looked after by Mrs. George Allen; and the old man wept every time he mentioned her name.

During the '60's, "Uncle Wash's" father drove a mail and passenger stage between Cusseta and LaFayette, Alabama - - and, finally died and was buried at LaFayette by the side of his wife. "Uncle Wash" "drifted over" to Columbus about fifty years ago and is now living with his two surviving children.

He has been married four times, all his wives dying "nachul" deaths. He has also "buried four chillun".

He was taught to read and write by the sons and daughters of Mr. George Allen, and attended church where a one-eyed white preacher -- named Mr. Terrentine -- preached to the slaves each Sunday "evenin'" (afternoon). The salary of this preacher was paid by Mr. George Allen.

When asked what this preacher usually preached about, "Uncle Wash" answered: "He was a one-eyed man an' couldn' see good; so, he mout a'made some mistakes, but he sho tole us plenty 'bout hell fire 'n brimstone."

"Uncle Wash" is a literal worshipper of the memory of his "old time white fokes."

Rev. W. B. Allen, Ex-Slave
425 -- Second Ave.
Columbus, Georgia.
(June 29, 1937)

In a second interview, the submission of which was voluntarily sought by himself, this very interesting specimen of a rapidly vanishing type expressed a desire to amend his previous interview (of May 10, 1937) to incorporate the following facts:

"For a number of years before freedom, my father bought his time from his master and traveled about over Russell County (Alabama) as a journeyman blacksmith, doing work for various planters and making good money - - as money went in those days - - on the side. At the close of the war, however, though he had a trunk full of Confederate money, all of his good money was gone.

Father could neither read nor write, but had a good head for figures and was very pious. His life had a wonderful influence upon me, though I was originally worldly - - that is, I drank and cussed, but haven't touched a drop of spirits in forty years and quit cussing before I entered the ministry in 1879.

I learned to pray when very young and kept it up even in my unsaved days. My white master's folks knew me to be a praying boy, and asked me -- in 1865 -- when the South was about whipped and General Wilson was headed our way - - to pray to God to hold the Yankees back. Of course, I didn't have any love for any Yankees -- and haven't now, for that matter -- but I told my white folks straight-from-the-shoulder that I could not pray along those lines. I told them flat-footedly that, while I loved them and would do any reasonable praying for them, I could not pray against my conscience: that I not only wanted to be free, but that I wanted to see all the Negroes freed!

I then told them that God was using the Yankees to scourge the slave-holders just as He had, centuries before, used heathens and outcasts to chastise His chosen people -- the Children of Israel."

(Here, it is to be noted that, for a slave boy of between approximately 15 and 17 years of age, remarkable familiarity with the Old Testament was displayed.)

The Parson then entered into a mild tirade against Yankees, saying:

"The only time the Northern people ever helped the Nigger was when they freed him. They are not friends of the Negro and many a time, from my pulpit, have I warned Niggers about going North. No, sir, the colored man doesn't belong in the North - - has no business up there, and you may tell the world that the Reverend W. B. Allen makes no bones about saying that! He also says that, if it wasn't for the influence of the white race in the South, the Negro race would revert to savagery within a year! Why, if they knew for dead certain that there was not a policeman or officer of the law in Columbus tonight, the good Lord only knows what they'd do tonight"!

When the good Parson had delivered himself as quoted, he was asked a few questions, the answers to which - - as shall follow -- disclose their nature.

"The lowest down Whites of slavery days were the average overseers. A few were gentlemen, one must admit, but the regular run of them were trash -- commoner than the 'poor white trash' - - and, if possible, their children were worse than their daddies. The name, 'overseer', was a synonym for 'slave driver', 'cruelty', 'brutishness'.
No, sir, a Nigger may be humble and refuse to talk outside of his race - - because he's afraid to, but you can't fool him about a white man!
And you couldn't fool him when he was a slave!
He knows a white man for what he is, and he knew him the same way in slavery times."

Concerning the punishment of slaves, the Reverend said:

"I never heard or knew of a slave being tried in court for any thing. I never knew of a slave being guilty of any crime more serious than taking something or violating plantation rules. And the only punishment that I ever heard or knew of being administered slaves was whipping.
I have personally known a few slaves that were beaten to death for one or more of the following offenses:
Leaving home without a pass,
Talking back to - - 'sassing' - - a white person,
Hitting another Negro,
Fussing, fighting, and rukkussing in the quarters,

Lying,

Loitering on their work,

Taking things - - the Whites called it stealing.

Plantation rules forbade a slave to:

Own a firearm,

Leave home without a pass,

Sell or buy anything without his master's consent,

Marry without his owner's consent,

Have a light in his cabin after a certain hour at night,

Attend any secret meeting,

Harbor or in any manner assist a runaway slave,

Abuse a farm animal,

Mistreat a member of his family, and do

A great many other things."

When asked if he had ever heard slaves plot an insurrection, the Parson answered in the negative.

When asked if he had personal knowledge of an instance of a slave offering resistance to corporal punishment, the Reverend shook his head, but said:

> "Sometimes a stripped Nigger would say some hard things to the white man with the strap in his hand, though he knew that he (the Negro) would pay for it dearly, for when a slave showed spirit that way the master or overseer laid the lash on all the harder."

When asked how the women took their whippings, he said:

> "They usually screamed and prayed, though a few never made a sound."

The Parson has had two wives and five children. Both wives and three of his children are dead. He is also now superannuated, but occasionally does a "little preaching", having only recently been down to Montezuma , Georgia, on a special call to deliver a message to the Methodist flock there.

Jack Atkinson - Ex-Slave

"Onct a man, twice a child," quoted Jack Atkinson, grey haired darkey, when being interviewed, "and I done started in my second childhood. I uster be active as a cat, but I ain't, no mo."

Jack acquired his surname from his white master, a Mr. Atkinson, who owned this Negro family prior to the War Between the States. He was a little boy during the war but remembers "refugeeing" to Griffin from Butts County, Georgia, with the Atkinsons when Sherman passed by their home on his march to the sea.

Jack's father, Tom, the body-servant of Mr. Atkinson, "tuk care of him" during the four years they were away at war. "Many's the time I done heard my daddy tell 'bout biting his hands he wuz so hongry, and him and Master drinking water outer the ruts of the road, they wuz so thirsty, during the war."

"Boss Man (Mr. Atkinson), wuz as fine man as ever broke bread", according to Jack.

When asked how he got married he stated that he "broke off a love vine and throwed it over the fence and if it growed" he would get married. The vine "just growed and growed" and it wasn't long before he and Lucy married.

"A hootin' owl is a sho sign of rain, and a screech owl means death, for a fact."

"A tree frog's holler is a true sign of rain."

Jack maintains that he has received "a second blessing from the Lord" and "no conjurer can bother him."

Jack Atkinson

Rt. D

Griffin, Georgia

Interviewed August 21, 1936

Unedited
Dis #5
100083
about 75
-85

EX TOWN SLAVE.
HANNAH AUSTIN.

When the writer was presented to Mrs. Hannah Austin she was immediately impressed with her alert youthful appearance. Mrs. Austin is well preserved for her age and speaks clearly and with much intelligence. The interview was a brief but interesting one. This was due partly to the fact that Mrs. Austin was a small child when The Civil War ended and too because her family was classed as "town slaves" so classed because of their superior intelligence.

Mrs. Austin was a child of ten or twelve years when the war ended. She doesn't know her exact age but estimated it to be between seventy and seventy five years. She was born the oldest child of Liza and George Hall. Their master Mr. Frank Hall was very kind to them and considerate in his treatment of them.

Briefly Mrs. Austin gave the following account of slavery as she knew it. "My family lived in a two room well built house which had many windows and a nice large porch. Our master, Mr. Hall was a merchant and operated a clothing store. Because Mr. Hall lived in town he did not need but a few slaves. My family which included my mother, father, sister, and myself were his only servants. Originally Mr. Hall did not own any slaves, however after marrying Mrs. Hall we were given to her by her father as a part of her inheritance.

My mother nursed Mrs. Hall, from a baby, consequently the Hall family was very fond of her and often made the statement that they woudl not part with her for anything in the workd, besides working as the cook for the Hall family my mother was also a fine seamstress and made clothing for the master's family and for our family. We were allowed an ample amount of good clothing which Mr. Hall selected from the stock in his store. My father worked as a porter in the store and did other jobs around the house. I did not have to work and spent most of my time playing with the Hall children. We were considered the better class of slaves and did not know the meaning of a hard time.

Other slave owners whipped their slaves severely and often, but I have never known our master to whip any one of my family. If any one in the family became ill the family doctor was called in as often as he was needed.

We did not have churches of our own but were allowed to attend the white churches in the afternoon. The White families attended in the forenoon. We seldom heard a true religious sermon; but were constantly preached the doctrine of obedience to our masters and mistresses. We were required to attend church every Sunday.

Marriages were conducted in much the same manner as they are today. After the usual courtship a minister was called in by the master and the marriage ceremony would then take place. In my opinion people of today are more lax in their attitude toward marriage than they were in those days. Following the marriage of a slave couple a celebration would take place often the master and his family would take part in the celebration.

I remember hearing my mother and father discuss the war; but was too young to know just the effect the war would have on the slave. One day I remember Mr. Hall coming to my mother telling her we were free. His exact words were quote - "Liza you don't belong to me any longer you belong to yourself. If you are hired now I will have to pay you. I do not want you to leave as you have a home here as long as you live." I watched my mother to see the effect his words would have on her and I saw her eyes fill with tears. Mr. Hall's eyes filled with tears also.

Soon after this incident a Yankee Army appeared in our village one day. They practically destroyed Mr. Hall's store by throwing all clothes and other merchandise into the streets. Seeing my sister and I they turned to us saying, "Little Negroes you are free there are no more masters and mistresses, here help yourseles to these clothes take them home with you. Not knowing any better we carried stockings, socks, dresses, underwear and many other pieces home. After this they opened the smoke house door and told us to go in and take all of the meat we wanted.

On another occasion the mistress called me asking that I come in the yard to play with the children". Here Mrs. Austin began to laugh and remarked "I did not go but politely told her I was free and didn't belong to any one but my mama and papa. As I spoke these words my mistress began to cry.

My mother and father continued to live with the Halls even after freedom and until their deaths. Although not impoverished most of the Hall's fortune was wiped out with the war".

Mrs. Austin married at the age of 16 years; and was the mother of four children, all of whom are dead. She was very ambitious and was determined to get an education if such was possible. After the war Northern white people came south and set up schools for the education of Negroes. She remembers the organization of the old Storrs School from which one of the pressnt Negroes Colleges Originated.

Mrs. Austin proudly spoke of her old blue back speller", which she still possesses; and of the days when she attended Storrs School.

As the writer made ready to depart Mrs. Austin smilingly informed her that she had told her all that she knew about slavery; and every word spoken was the truth.

[redacted]

" A FEW FACTS OF SLAVERY"

As Told by Celestia Avery-ExSlave

Mrs. Celestia Avery is a small mulatto woman about 5 ft. in height. She has a remarkably clear memory in view of the fact that she is about 75 years of age. Before the interview began she reminded the writer that the facts to be related were either told to her by her grandmother, Sylvia Heard, or were facts which she remembered herself.

Mrs. Avery was born 75 years ago in Troupe County, LaGrange, Ga. the eighth oldest child of Lenora and Silas Heard. There were 10 other children beside herself. She and her family were owned by Mr. & Mrs. Peter Heard. In those days the slaves carried the surname of their master; this accounted for all slaves having the same name whether they were kin or not.

The owner Mr. Heard had a plantation of about 500 acres and was considered wealthy by all who knew him. Mrs. Avery was unable to give the exact number of slaves on the plantation, but knew he owned a large number. Cotton, corn, peas, potatoes, (etc.) were the main crops raised.

The homes provided for the slaves were two room log cabins which had one door and one window. These homes were not built in a group together but were more or less scattered over the plantation. Slave homes were very imple and only contained a home made table, chair and bed which were made of the same type of wood and could easily be cleaned by scouring with sand every Saturday. The beds were bottomed with rope which was run backward and forward from one rail to the other. On this framework was placed a mattress of wheat straw. Each spring the mattresses were emptied and refilled with fresh wheat straw.

Slaves were required to prepare their own meals three times a day. This was done in a big open fire place which was filled with hot coals. The master did not give them much of a variety of food, but allowed each family to raise their own vegetables. Each family was given a hand out of bacon and meal on Saturdays and through the week.corn ash cakes and meat; which had been broiled on the hot coals was the usual diet found in each home. The diet did not vary even at Christmas only a little fruit was added.

Each family was provided with a loom and in Mrs. Avery's family, her grandmother, Sylvia Heard, did most of the carding and spinning of the thread into cloth. The most common cloth for women clothes was homespun, and calico. This same cloth was dyed and used to make men shirts and pants. Dye was prepared by taking a berry known as the shumake berry and boiling them with walnut peelings. Spring and fall were the seasons for masters to give shoes and clothing to their slaves. Both men and women wore brogan shoes, the only difference being the piece in the side of the womens.

One woman was required to do the work around the house there was also one slave man required to work around the house doing odd jobs. Other than these two every one else was required to do the heavy work in the fields. Work began at "sun up" and lasted until "sun down". In the middle of the day the big bell was rung to summon the workers from the field, for their mid-day lunch. After work hours slaves were then free to dow work around their own cabins, such as sewing, cooking (etc.)

"Once a week Mr. Heard allowed his slaves to have a frolic and folks would get broke down from so much dancing" Mrs. Avery remarked. The music was furnished with fiddles. When asked how the slaves came to own fiddles she replied, "They bought them with money they earned selling chickens." At night slaves would steal off from the Heard plantation, go to LaGrange, Ga. and sell chickens which they had raised. Of course the masters always required half of every thing raised by each slave and it was not permissible for any slave to sell anything. Another form of entertainment was the quilting party.

Every one would go together to different person's home on each separate night of the week and finish that person's quilts. Each night this was repeated until every one had a sufficient amount of covering for the winter. Any slave from another plantation, desiring to attend these frolics, could do so after securing a pass from their master.

Mrs. Avery related the occasion when her Uncle William was caught off the Heard plantation without a pass, and was whipped almost to death by the "Pader Rollers." He stole off to the depths of thw woods here he built a cave large enough to live in. A few nights later he came back to the plantation unobserved and carried his wife and two children back to this cave where they lived until after freedom. When found years later his wife had given birth to two children. No one was ever able to find his hiding place and if he saw any one in the woods he would run like a lion.

Mr. Heard was a very mean master and was not liked by any one of his slaves. Secretly each one hated him. He whipped unmercifully and in most cases unnecessarily. However, he sometimes found it hard to subdue some slaves who happened to have very high tempers. In the event this was the case he would set a pack of hounds on him. Mrs. Avery related to the writer the story told to her of Mr. Heard's cruelty by her grandmother. The facts were as follows: "Every morning my grandmother would pray, and old man Heard despised to hear any one pray saying they were only doing so that they might become free niggers. Just as sure as the sun would rise, she would get a whipping; but this did not stop her prayers every morning before day. This particular time grandmother Sylvia was in "family way" and that morning she began to pray as usual. The master heard her and became so angry he came to her cabin siezed and pulled her clothes from her body and tied her to a young sapling. He whipped her so brutally that her body was raw all over. When darkness fell her husband cut her down from the tree, during the day he was afraid to go near her. Rather than go back to the cabin she crawled on her knees to the woods and her husband brought grease for her to grease her raw body. For two weeks the master hunted but could not find her; however, when he finally did, she had given birth to twins. The only thing that saved her was the fact that she was a mid-wife and always carried a small pin knife which she used to cut the navel cord of the babies. After doing this she tore her petticoat into two pieces and wrapped each baby." Grandmother Sylvia lived to get 115 years old.

Not only was Mr. Henderson cruel but it seemed that every one he hired in the capacity of overseer was just as cruel. For instance, Mrs. Henderson's grandmother Sylvia, was told to take her clothes off when she reached the end of a row. She was to be whipped because she had not completed the required amount of hoeing for the day. Grandmother continued hoeing until she came to a fence; as the overweer reached out to grab her she snatched a fence railing and broke it across his arms. On another occasion grandmother Sylvia ran all the way to town to tell the master that an overseer was beating her husband to death. The master immediately jumped on his horse and started for home; and reaching the plantation he ordered the overseer to stop whipping the old man. Mrs. Avery received one whipping, with a hair brush, for disobedience; this was given to her by the mistress.

Slaves were given separate churches, but the minister, who conducted the services, was white. Very seldom did the text vary from the usual one of obedience to the master and mistress, and the necessity for good behavior. Every one was required to attend church , however, the only self expression they could indulge in without conflict with the master was that of singing. Any one heard praying was given a good whipping; for most masters thought their prayers no good since freedom was the uppermost thought in every one's head.

On the Heard plantation as on a number of others, marriages were made by the masters of the parties concerned. Marriage licenses were unheard of. If both masters mutually consented, the marriage ceremony was considered over with. After that the husband was given a pass to visit his wife once a week. In the event children were born the naming of them was left entirely to the master. Parents were not allowed to name them.

Health of slaves was very important to every slave owner for loss of life meant loss of money to them. Consequently they would call in their family doctor, if a slave became seriously ill. In minor cases of illness home remedies were used. "In fact," Mrs. Avery smilingly remarked, "We used every thing for medicine that grew in the ground." One particular home remedy was known as "Cow foot oil" which was made by boiling cow's feet in water. Other medicines used were hoarhound tea, catnip tea, and castor oil. Very often medicines and doctors failed to save life; and whenever a slave died he was buried the same day. Mrs. Avery remarked, "If he died before dinner the funeral and burial usually took place immediately after dinner."

Although a very young child, Mrs. Avery remembers the frantic attempt slave owners made to hide their money; when the war broke out. The following is a story related concerning the Heard family. "Mr. Heard, our master, went to the swamp, dug a hole, and hid his money, then he and his wife left for town on their horses. My oldest brother, Percy, saw their hiding place; and when the Yanks came looking for the money, he carried them straight to the swamps and showed them where the money was hidden.) Although the Yeard farm was in the country the highway was very near and Mrs. Avery told of the long army of soldiers marching to La Grange singing the following song: "Rally around the flag boys, rally around the flag, joy, joy, for freedom." When the war ended Mr. Heard visited every slave home and broke the news to each family that they were free people and if they so desired could remain on his plantation. Mrs. Avery's family moved away, in fact most slave families did, for old man Heard had been such a cruel master everyone was anxious to get away from him. However, one year later he sold his plantation to Mr George Traylor and some of the families moved back, Mrs. Avery's family included.

Mrs. Avery married at the age of 16; and was the mother of 14 children, three of whom are still living. Although she has had quite a bit of illness, during her life, at present she is quite well and active in spite of her old age. She assured the writer that the story of slavery, which she had given her, was a true one and sincerely hoped it would do some good in this world.

FOLKLORE

(Negro)

In a small house at 173 Phoenix Alley, N.E. lives a little old woman about 5 ft. 2 in. in height, who is an ex-slave. She greeted the writer with a bright smile and bade her enter and have a seat by the small fire in the poorly lighted room. The writer vividly recalled the interview she gave on slavery previously and wondered if any facts concerning superstitions, conjure, signs, etc. could be obtained from her. After a short conversation pertaining to everyday occurrences, the subject of superstition was broached to Mrs. Avery. The idea amused her and she gave the writer the following facts: As far as possible the stories are given in her exact words. The interview required two days, November 30 and December 2, 1936.

"When you see a dog lay on his stomach and slide it is a true sign of death. This is sho true cause it happened to me. Years ago when I lived on Pine Street I was sitting on my steps playing with my nine-months old baby. A friend uv mine came by and sat down; and as we set there a dog that followed her began to slide on his stomach. It scared me; and I said to her, did you see that dog? Yes, I sho did. That night my baby died and it wusn't sick at all that day. That's the truth and a sho sign of death. Anudder sign of death is ter dream of a new-born baby. One night not so long ago I dreamt about a new-born baby and you know I went ter the door and called Miss Mary next door and told her I dreamed about a new-born baby, and she said, Oh! that's a sho sign of death. The same week that gal's baby over there died. It didn't surprise me when I heard it cause I knowed somebody round here wus go die." She continued:

"Listen, child! If ebber you clean your bed, don't you never sweep off your springs with a broom. Always wipe 'em with a rag, or use a brush. Jest as sho as you do you see an experience death around you. I took my bed down and swept off my springs, and I jest happened to tell old Mrs. Smith; and she jumped up and said, "Child, you ought not done that cause it's a sign of death.' Sho nuff the same night I lost another child that wuz eight years old. The child had heart trouble, I think."

Mrs. Avery believes in luck to a certain extent. The following are examples of how you may obtain luck:

"I believe you can change your luck by throwing a teaspoonful of sulphur in the fire at zackly 12 o'clock in the day. I know last week I was sitting here without a bit of fire, but I wuzn't thinking 'bout doing that till a 'oman came by and told me ter scrape up a stick fire and put a spoonful of sulphur on it; and sho nuff in a hour's time a coal man came by and gave me a tub uv coal. Long time ago I used ter work fer some white women and every day at 12 o'clock I wuz told ter put a teaspoonful of sulphur in the fire."

"Another thing, I sho ain't going ter let a 'oman come in my house on Monday morning unless a man done come in there fust. No, surree, if it seem lak one ain't coming soon, I'll call one of the boy chilluns, jest so it is a male. The reason fer this is cause women is bad luck."

The following are a few of the luck charms as described by Mrs. Avery:

"Black cat bone is taken from a cat. First, the cat is killed and boiled, after which the meat is scraped from the bones. The bones are then taken to the creek and thrown in. The bone that goes up stream is the lucky bone and is the one that should be kept." "There is a boy in this neighborhood that sells liquor and I know they done locked him up ten or twelve times but he always git out. They say he carries a black cat bone," related Mrs. Avery.

"The Devil's shoe string looks jest like a fern with a lot of roots. My mother used to grow them in the corner of our garden. They are lucky.

"Majres (?) are always carried tied in the corner of a handkerchief. I don't know how they make 'em.

"I bought a lucky stick from a man onct. It looked jest lak a candle, only it wuz small; but he did have some sticks as large as candles and he called them lucky sticks, too, but you had to burn them all night in your room. He also had some that looked jest lak buttons, small and round."

The following are two stories of conjure told by Mrs. Avery:

"I knowed a man onct long ago and he stayed sick all der time. He had the headache from morning till night. One day he went to a old man that wuz called a conjurer; this old man told him that somebody had stole the sweat-band out of his cap and less he got it back, something terrible would happen. They say this man had been going with a 'oman and she had stole his sweat-band. Well, he never did get it, so he died.

"I had a cousin named Alec Heard, and he had a wife named Anna Heard. Anna stayed sick all der time almost;fer two years she complained. One day a old conjurer came to der house and told Alec that Anna wuz poisoned, but if he would give him $5.00 he would come back Sunday morning and find the conjure. Alec wuz wise, so he bored a hole in the kitchen floor so that he could jest peep through there to der back steps. Sho nuff Sunday morning the nigger come back and as Alec watched him he dug down in the gound a piece, then he took a ground puppy, threw it in the hole and covered it up. All right, he started digging again and all at onct he jumped up and cried: 'Here 'tis! I got it.'" 'Got what?' Alec said, running to the door with a piece of board. 'I got the ground puppy dat wuz buried fer her.' Alec wuz so mad he jumped on that man and beat him most to death. They say he did that all the time and kept a lot of ground puppies fer that purpose." Continuing, she explained that a ground puppy was a worm with two small horns. They are dug up out of the ground, and there is a belief that you will die if one barks at you.

Mrs. Avery related two ways in which you can keep from being conjured by anyone.

"One thing I do every morning is ter sprinkle chamber-lye (urine) with salt and then throw it all around my door. They sho can't fix you if you do this. Anudder thing, if you wear a silver dime around your leg they can't fix you. The 'oman live next door says she done wore two silver dimes around her leg for 18 years."

Next is a story of the Jack O'Lantern.

"Onct when I wuz a little girl a lot of us chillun used to slip off and take walnuts from a old man. We picked a rainy night so nobody would see us, but do you know it looked like a thousand Jack ma' Lanterns got in behind us. They wuz all around us. I never will ferget my brother telling me ter get out in the path and turn my pocket wrong side out. I told him I didn't have no pocket but the one in my apron; he said,'well,turn that one wrong side out.' Sho nuff we did and they scattered then."

Closing the interview, Mrs. Avery remarked: "That's bout all I know; but come back some time and maybe I'll think of something else."

On December 3 and 4, 1936, Mrs. Emmaline Heard was interviewed at her home, 239 Cain Street. The writer had visited Mrs. Heard previously, and it was at her own request that another visit was made. This visit was supposed to be one to obtain information and stories on the practice of conjure. On two previous occasions Mrs. Heard's stories had proved very interesting, and I knew as I sat there waiting for her to begin that she had something very good to tell me. She began:

"Chile, this story wuz told ter me by my father and I know he sho wouldn't lie. Every word of it is the trufe; fact, everything I ebber told you wuz the trufe. Now, my pa had a brother, old Uncle Martin, and his wife wuz name Julianne. Aunt Julianne used ter have spells and fight and kick all the time. They had doctor after doctor but none did her any good. Somebody told Uncle Martin to go ter a old conjurer and let the doctors go cause they wan't doing nothing fer her anyway. Sho nuff he got one ter come see her and give her some medicine. This old man said she had bugs in her head, and after giving her the medicine he started rubbing her head. While he rubbed her head he said: 'Dar's a bug in her head; it looks jest like a big black roach. Now, he's coming out of her head through her ear; whatever you do, don't let him get away cause I want him. Whatever you do, catch him; he's going ter run, but when he hits the pillow, grab 'em. I'm go take him and turn it back on the one who is trying ter send you ter the grave.' Sho nuff that bug drap out her ear and flew; she hollered, and old Uncle Martin ran in the room, snatched the bed clothes off but they never did find him. Aunt Julianne never did get better and soon she died. The conjurer said if they had a caught the bug she would a lived."

The next story is a true story. The facts as told by Mrs. Heard were also witnessed by her; as it deals with the conjuring of one of her sons. It is related in her exact words as nearly as possible.

"I got a son named Albert Heard. He is living and well; but chile, there wuz a time when he wuz almost ter his grave. I wuz living in town them, and Albert and his wife wuz living in the country with their two chillun. Well, Albert got down sick and he would go ter doctors, and go ter doctors, but they didn't do him any good. I wuz worried ter death cause I had ter run backards and for'ards and it wuz a strain on me. He waz suffering with a knot on his right side and he couldn't even fasten his shoes cause it pained him so, and it wuz so bad he couldn't even button up his pants. A 'oman teached school out there by the name of Mrs. Yancy; she's dead now but she lived right here on Randolph Street years ago. Well, one day when I wuz leaving Albert's house I met her on the way from her school. 'Good evening, Mrs. Heard,' she says. 'How is Mr. Albert?' I don't hardly know, I says, cause he don't get no better. She looked at me kinda funny and said, don't you believe he's hurt?' Yes mam, I said, I sho do. 'Well,' says she, 'I been wanting to say something to you concerning this but I didn't know how you would take it. If I tell you somewhere ter go will you go, and tell them I sent you?' Yes mam, I will do anything if Albert can get better. 'All right then', she says. 'Catch the Federal Prison car and get off at Butler St.' In them days that car came down Forrest Ave. 'When you get to Butler St.', she says, 'walk up to Clifton St. and go to such and such a number. Knock on the door and a 'oman by the name of Mrs. Hirshpath will come ter the door. Fore she let you in she go ask who sent you there; when you tell 'er, she'll let you in. Now lemme tell you she keeps two quarts of whisky all the time and you have ter drink a little with her; sides that she cusses nearly every word she speaks; but don't let that scare you; she will sho get your son up if it kin be done.' Sho nuff that old 'oman did jest lak Mrs. Yancy said she would do. She had a harsh voice and she spoke right snappy. When she let me in she said, sit down. You lak whisky?' I said, well, I take a little dram sometimes. 'Well, here take some of this', she said. I poured a little bit and drank it kinda lak I wuz afraid. She cursed and said 'I ain't go conjure you. Drink it.' She got the cards and told me to cut 'em, so I did. Looking at the cards, she said: 'You lak ter wait too long; they got him marching to the cemetery. The poor thing! I'll fix those devils. (A profane word was used instead of devils). He got a knot on his side, ain't he?' Yes, Mam, I said. That 'oman told me everything that was wrong with Albert and zackly how he acted. All at once she said: 'If them d_____d things had hatched in him it would a been too late. If you do zackly lak I tell you I'll get him up from there.' I sho will, I told her. 'Well, there's a stable sets east of his house. His house got three rooms and a path go straight to the stable. I see it there where he hangs his harness. Yes, I see it all, the devils! Have you got any money?' Yes, mam, a little, I said. 'All right then,'she said. 'Go to the drug store and get 5¢ worth of blue stone; 5¢ wheat bran; and go ter a fish market and ask 'em ter give you a little fish brine; then go in the woods and get some poke-root berries. Now, there's two kinds of poke-root berries, the red skin and the white skin berry. Put all this in a pot, mix with it the guts from a green gourd and 9 parts of red pepper. Make a poultice and put to his side on that knot. Now, listen, your son will be afraid and think you are trying ter do something ter him but be gentle and persuade him that its fer his good.' Child, he sho did act funny when I told him I wanted to treat his side. I had ter tell him I wuz carrying out doctors orders so he could get well. He reared and fussed and said he didn't want that mess on him. I told him the doctor says you do very well till you go ter the horse lot then you go blind and you can't see. He looked at me. 'Sho nuff, Ma, he said, 'that sho is the trufe. I have ter always call one of the chillun when I go there cause I can't see how ter get back ter the house.' Well, that convinced him and he let me fix the medicine for him. I put him ter bed and made the poultice, then I put it ter his side. Now this 'oman said no one wuz ter take it off the next morning but me. I wuz suppose ter fix three, one each night, and after taking each one off ter bury it lak dead folks is buried, east and west, and ter make a real grave out of each one. Well, when I told him not ter move it the next morning, but let me move it, he got funny again and wanted to know why. Do you know I had ter play lak I could move it without messing up my bed clothes and if he moved it he might waste it all. Finally he said he would call me the next morning. Sho nuff, the next morning he called me, ma! ma! come take it off. I went in the room and he wuz smiling. I slept all night long he said, and I feel so much better. I'm so glad, I said, and do you know he could reach down and fasten up his shoe and it had been a long time since he could do that. Later that day I slipped out and made my first grave under the fig bush in the garden. I even put up head boards, too. That night Albert said, 'Mama, fix another one. I feel so much better.' I sho will, I said. Thank God you're better; so fer three nights I fixed poultices and put ter his side and each morning he would tell me how much better he felt. Then the last morning I wuz fixing breakfast and he sat in the next room. After while Albert jumped up and hollered, Ma! Ma!' What is it, 'I said. 'Mama, that knot is gone. It dropped down in my pants.' What! I cried. Where is it? Chile, we looked but we didn't find anything, but the know had sho gone. Der 'oman had told me ter come back when the knot moved and she would tell me what else ter do. That same day I went ter see her and when I told her she just shouted, 'I fixed 'em, The devils! Now, says she, do you know where you can get a few leaves off a yellow peachtree? It must be a yellow peach tree, though. Yes, mam, I says to her. I have a yellow peachtree right there in my yard. Well, she says, get a handful of leaves, then take a knife and scrape the bark up, then make a tea and give him so it will heal up the poison from that knot in his side, also mix a few jimson weeds with it. I come home and told him I wanted ter give him a tea. He got scared and said, what fer, Ma? I had ter tell him I wuz still carrying out the doctor's orders. Well, he let me give him the tea and that boy got well. I went back to Mrs. Hirshpath and told her my son was well and I wanted to pay her. Go on, she said, keep the dollar and send your chillun ter school. This sho happened ter me and I know people kin fix you. Yes sir.

The next story was told to Mrs. Heard by Mrs. Hirspath, the woman who cured her son.

I used to go see that 'oman quite a bit and even sent some of my friends ter her. One day while I wuz there she told me about this piece of work she did.

"There wuz a young man and his wife and they worked fer some white folks. They had jest married and wuz trying ter save some money ter buy a home with. All at onct the young man went blind and it almost run him and his wife crazy cause they didn't know what in the world ter do. Well, somebody told him and her about Mrs. Hirshpath, so they went ter see her. One day, says Mrs. Hirshpath, a big fine carriage drew up in front of her door and the coachman helped him to her door. She asked him who sent him and he told her. She only charged 50¢ for giving advice and after you wuz cured it wuz up ter you to give her what you wanted to. Well, this man gave her 50¢ and she talked ter him. She says, boy, you go home and don't you put that cap on no more. What cap? he says. That cap you wears ter clean up the stables with, cause somebody done dressed that cap fer you, and every time you perspire and it run down ter your eyes it makes you blind. You jest get that cap and bring it ter me. I'll fix 'em; they's trying ter make you blind, but I go let you see. The boy was overjoyed, and sho nuff he went back and brought her that cap, and it wuzn't long fore he could see good as you and me. He brought that 'oman $50, but she wouldn't take but $25 and give the other $25 back ter him.

"What I done told you is the trufe, every word of it; I know some other things that happened but you come back anudder day fer that."

PLANTATION LIFE

Interview with:

GEORGIA BAKER
369 Meigs Street
Athens, Georgia

Written by: Mrs. Sadie B. Hornsby (white)
Athens -

Edited by: Mrs. Sarah H. Hall
Athens -

and

John N. Booth
Dist. Supvr.
Federal Writers' Project
Residencies 6 & 7
Augusta, Ga.

August 4, 1938

GEORGIA BAKER
Ex-Slave - Age 87.

Georgia's address proved to be the home of her daughter, Ida Baker. The clean-swept walks of the small yard were brightened by borders of gay colored zinnias and marigolds in front of the drab looking two-story, frame house. "Come in," answered Ida, in response to a knock at the front door. "Yessum, Mammy's here. Go right in dat dere room and you'll find her."

Standing by the fireplace of the next room was a thin, very black woman engaged in lighting her pipe. A green checked gingham apron partially covered her faded blue frock over which she wore a black shirtwaist fastened together with "safety first" pins. A white cloth, tied turban fashion about her head, and gray cotton hose worn with black and white slippers that were run down at the heels, completed her costume.

"Good mornin'. Yessum, dis here's Georgia," was her greeting. "Let's go in dar whar Ida is so us can set down. I don't know what you come for, but I guess I'll soon find out."

Georgia was eager to talk but her articulation had been impaired by a paralytic stroke and at times it was difficult to understand her jumble of words. After observance of the amenities; comments on the weather, health and such subjects, she began:

"Whar was I born? Why I was born on de plantation of a great man. It was Marse Alec Stephens' plantation 'bout a mile and a half from Crawfordville, in Taliaferro County. Mary and Grandison Tilly was my Ma and Pa. Ma was cook up at de big house and she died when I was jus' a little gal. Pa was a field hand, and he belonged to Marse Britt Tilly.

"Dere was four of us chillun: me, and Mary, and Frances, and Mack," she counted on the fingers of one hand. "Marse Alec let Marse Jim Johnson have Mack for his bodyguard. Frances, she wuked in de field, and Mary was de baby - she was too little to wuk. Me, I was 14 years old when de War was over. I swept yards, toted water to de field, and played 'round de house and yard wid de rest of de chillun.

"De long, log houses what us lived in was called "shotgun" houses 'cause dey had three rooms, one behind de other in a row lak de barrel of a shotgun. All de chillun slept in one end room and de grown folkses slept in de other end room. De kitchen whar us cooked and et was de middle room. Beds was made out of pine poles put together wid cords. Dem wheat-straw mattresses was for grown folkses mostly 'cause nigh all de chillun slept on pallets. How-some-ever, dere was some few slave chillun what had beds to sleep on. Pillows! Dem days us never knowed what pillows was. Gals slept on one side of de room and boys on de other in de chilluns room. Uncle Jim, he was de bed-maker, and he made up a heap of little beds lak what dey calls cots now.

"Becky and Stafford Stephens was my Grandma and Grandpa. Marse Alec bought 'em in Old Virginny. I don't know what my Grandma done 'cause she died 'fore I was borned, but I 'members Grandpa Stafford well enough. I can see him now. He was a old man what slept on a trundle bed in the kitchen, and all he done was to set by de fire all day wid a switch in his hand and tend de chillun whilst dere mammies was at wuk. Chillun minded better dem days dan dey does now. Grandpa Stafford never had to holler at 'em but one time. Dey knowed dey would git de switch next if dey didn't behave.

"Now dere you is axin' 'bout dat somepin' t'eat us had dem days! Ida, ain't dere a piece of watermelon in de ice box?" Georgia lifted the lid of a small ice box, got out a piece of melon, and began to smack her thick lips as she devoured it with an air of ineffable satisfaction. When she had tilted the rind to swallow the last drop of pink juice, she indicated that she was fortified and ready to exercise her now well lubricated throat, by resuming her story:

"Oh, yessum! Marse Alec, had plenty for his slaves to eat. Dere was meat, bread, collard greens, snap beans, 'taters, peas, all sorts of dried fruit, and just lots of milk and butter. Marse Alec had 12 cows and dat's whar I learned to love milk so good. De same Uncle Jim what made our beds made our wooden bowls what dey kept filled wid bread and milk for de chillun all day. You might want to call dat place whar Marse

Alec had our veg'tables raised a gyarden, but it looked more lak a big field to me, it was so big. You jus' ought to have seed dat dere fireplace whar dey cooked all us had to eat. It was one sho 'nough big somepin, all full of pots, skillets, and ovens. Dey warn't never 'lowed to git full of smut neither. Dey had to be cleant and shined up atter evvy meal, and dey sho was pretty hangin' dar in dat big old fireplace.

"George and Mack was de hunters. When dey went huntin' dey brought back jus' evvything: possums, rabbits, coons, squirrels, birds, and wild turkeys. Yessum, wild turkeys is same sort of birds I reckon, but when us talked about birds to eat us meant part'idges. Some folkses calls 'em quails. De fishes us had in summertime was a sight to see. Us sho et good dem days. Now us jus' eats what-some-ever us can git.

"Summertime us jus' wore what us wanted to. Dresses was made wid full skirts gathered on to tight fittin' waisties. Winter clothes was good and warm; dresses made of yarn cloth made up jus' lak dem summertime clothes, and petticoats and draw's made out of osnaburg. Chillun what was big enough done de spinnin' and Aunt Betsey and Aunt Tinny, dey wove most evvy night 'til dey rung de bell at 10:00 o'clock for us to go to bed. Us made bolts and bolts of cloth evvy year.

"Us went bar'foots in summer, but bless your sweet life us had good shoes in winter and wore good stockin's too. It tuk three shoemakers for our plantation. Dey was Uncle Isom, Uncle Jim, and Uncle Stafford. Dey made up hole-stock shoes for de 'omans and gals and brass-toed brogans for de mens and boys.

"Us had pretty white dresses for Sunday. Marse Alec wanted evvybody on his place dressed up dat day. He sont his houseboy, Uncle Harris, down to de cabins evvy Sunday mornin' to tell evvy slave to clean hisself up, Dey warn't never give no change to forgit. Dere was a big old room sot aside for a wash-room. Folkses laughs at me now 'cause I ain't never stopped takin' a bath evvy Sunday mornin'.

"Marse Lordnorth Stephens was de boss on Marse Alec's plantation. Course Marse Alec owned us and he was our sho 'nough Marster. Neither one of 'em ever married. Marse Lordnorth was a good man, but he didn't have no use for 'omans - he was a sissy. Dere warn't no Marster no whar no better dan our Marse Alec Stephens, but he never stayed home enough to tend to things hisself much 'cause he was all de time too busy on de outside. He was de President or somepin of our side durin' de war.

"Uncle Pierce went wid Marse Alec evvy whar he went. His dog, Rio, had more sense dan most folkses. Marse

Alec, he was all de time havin' big mens visit him up at de big house. One time, out in de yard, him and one of dem 'portant mens got in a argyment 'bout somepin. Us chillun snuck up close to hear what dey was makin' such a rukus 'bout. I heared Marse Alec say: 'I got more sense in my big toe dan you is got in your whole body.' And he was right - he did have more sense dan most folkses. Ain't I been a-tellin' you he was de President or somepin lak dat, dem days?

" Ma, she was Marse Alec's cook and looked atter de house. Atter she died Marse Lordnorth got Mrs. Mary Berry from Habersham County to keep house at de big house, but Aunt 'Liza, she done de cookin' atter Miss Mary got dar. Us little Niggers sho' did love Miss Mary. Us called her "Mammy Mary" sometimes. Miss Mary had three sons and one of 'em was named Jeff Davis. I 'members when dey come and got him and tuk him off to war. Marse Lordnorth built a four-room house on de plantation for Miss Mary and her boys. Evvybody loved our Miss Mary, 'cause she was so good and sweet, and dere warn't nothin' us wouldn't have done for her.

"No Lord! Marse Lordnorth never needed no overseer or no carriage driver neither. Uncle Jim was de head man what got de Niggers up evvy mornin' and started 'em off to wuk right. De big house sho was a pretty place, a-settin' up on a high hill. De squirrels was so tame dar dey jus' played all 'round de yard. Marse Alec's dog is buried in dat yard.

"No Mam, I never knowed how many acres dere was in de plantation us lived on, and Marse Alec had other places too. He had land scattered evvywhar. Lord, dere was a heap of Niggers on dat place, and all of us was kin to one another. Grandma Becky and Grandpa Stafford was de fust slaves Marse Alec ever had, and dey sho had a passel of chillun. One thing sho Marse Lordnorth wouldn't keep no bright colored Nigger on dat plantation if he could help it. Aunt Mary was a bright colored Nigger and dey said dat Marse John, Marse Lordnorth's brother, was her Pa, but anyhow Marse Lordnorth never had no use for her 'cause she was a bright colored Nigger.

"Marse Lordnorth never had no certain early time for his slaves to git up nor no special late time for 'em to quit wuk. De hours dey wuked was 'cordin' to how much wuk was ahead to be done. Folks in Crawfordville called us 'Stephens' Free Niggers.'

"Us minded Marse Lordnorth - us had to do dat - but he let us do pretty much as us pleased. Us never had no sorry piece of a Marster. He was a good man and he made a sho 'nough good Marster. I never seed no Nigger git a beatin', and what's more I never heared of nothin' lak dat on our place. Dere was a jail in Crawfordville, but none of us Niggers on Marse Alec's place warn't never put in it.

"No Lord! None of us Niggers never knowed nothin' 'bout readin' and writin'. Dere warn't no school for

Niggers den, and I ain't never been to school a day in my life. Niggers was more skeered of newspapers dan dey is of snakes now, and us never knowed what a Bible was dem days.

"Niggers never had no churches of deir own den. Dey went to de white folkses' churches and sot in de gallery. One Sunday when me and my sister Frances went to church I found 50¢ in Confederate money and showed it to her. She tuk it away from me. Dat's de onliest money I seed durin' slavery time. Course you knows dey throwed Confederate money away for trash atter de war was over. Den us young chaps used to play wid it.

"I never went to no baptizin's nor no funerals neither den. Funerals warn't de style. When a Nigger died dem days, dey jus' put his body in a box and buried it. I 'members very well when Aunt Sallie and Aunt Catherine died, but I was little den, and I didn't take it in what dey done 'bout buryin' 'em.

"None of Marse Alec's slaves never run away to de North, 'cause he was so good to 'em dey never wanted to leave him. De onliest Nigger what left Marse Alec's place was Uncle Dave, and he wouldn't have left 'cept he got in trouble wid a white 'oman. You needn't ax me her name 'cause I ain't gwine to tell it, but I knows it well as I does my own name. Anyhow Marse Alec give Uncle Dave some money and told him to leave, and nobody never seed him no more atter dat.

"Oh yessum! Us heared 'bout 'em, but none of us never seed no patterollers on Marse Alec's plantation. He never 'lowed 'em on his land, and he let 'em know dat he kept his slaves supplied wid passes whenever dey wanted to go places so as dey could come and go when dey got good and ready. Thursday and Sadday nights was de main nights dey went off. Uncle Stafford's wife was Miss Mary Stephen's cook, Uncle Jim's wife lived on de Finley place, and Uncle Isom's belonged to de Hollises, so dey had regular passes all de time and no patterollers never bothered 'em none.

"Whenever Marse Alec or Marse Lordnorth wanted to send a message dey jus' put George or Mack on a horse and sont 'em on but one thing sho, dere warn't no slave knowed what was in dem letters.

"Marse Alec sho had plenty of mules. Some of 'em was named: Pete, Clay, Rollin, Jack, and Sal. Sal was Allen's plow mule, and he set a heap of store by her. Dere was a heap more mules on dat place, but I can't call back dere names right now.

"Most times when slaves went to deir quarters at night, mens rested, but sometimes dey holped de 'omans cyard de cotton and wool. Young folkses frolicked, sung songs, and visited from cabin to cabin. When dey got behind wid de field wuk, sometimes slaves wuked atter dinner Saddays, but dat warn't often. But, Oh, dem Sadday nights! Dat was when slaves got together and danced. George, he blowed de quills, and he sho could blow grand dance music on 'em. Dem Niggers would jus' dance down. Dere warn't no foolishment 'lowed atter 10:00 o'clock no night. Sundays dey went to church and visited 'round, but folks didn't spend as much time gaddin' 'bout lak dey does now days.

"Christmas Day! Oh, what a time us Niggers did have dat day! Marse Lordnorth and Marse Alec give us evvything you could name to eat:cake of all kinds, fresh meat, lightbread, turkeys, chickens, ducks, geese, and all kinds of wild game. Dere was allus plenty of pecans, apples, and dried peaches too at Christmas. Marse Alec had some trees what had fruit dat looked lak bananas on 'em, but I done forgot what was de name of dem trees. Marse Alec would call de grown folkses to de big house early in de mornin' and pass 'round a big pewter pitcher full of whiskey, den he would put a little whiskey in dat same pitcher and fill it wid sweetened water and give dat to us chillun. Us called dat 'toddy' or 'dram'. Marse Alex allus had plenty of good whiskey, 'cause Uncle Willis made it up for him and it was made jus' right. De night atter Christmas Day us pulled syrup candy, drunk more liquor, and danced. Us had a big time for a whole week and den on New Year's Day us done a little wuk jus' to start de year right and us feasted dat day on fresh meat, plenty of cake, and whiskey. Dere was allus a big pile of ash-roasted 'taters on hand to go wid dat good old baked meat. Us allus tried to raise enough 'taters to last all through de winter 'cause Niggers sho does love dem sweet 'taters. No Mam, us never knowed nothin' 'bout Santa

Claus 'til atter de war.

"No Mam, dere warn't no special cornshuckin's and cotton pickin's on Marse Alec's place, but of course dey did quilt in de winter 'cause dere had to be lots of quiltin' done for all dem slaves to have plenty of warm kivver, and you knows, Lady, 'omans can quilt better if dey gits a passel of 'em together to do it. Marse Alec and Marse Lordnorth never 'lowed dere slaves to mix up wid other folkses business much.

"Oh Lord! Us never played no games in slavery times, 'cept jus' to run around in a ring and pat our hands. I never sung no songs 'cause I warn't no singer, and don't talk 'bout no Raw Head and Bloody Bones or nothin' lak dat. Dey used to skeer us chillun so bad 'bout dem sort of things dat us used to lay in bed at night a-shakin' lak us was havin' chills. I've seed plenty of ha'nts right here in Athens. Not long atter I had left Crawfordville and moved to Athens, I had been in bed jus' a little while one night, and was jus' dozin' off to sleep when I woke up and sot right spang up in bed. I seed a white man, dressed in white, standin' before me. I sho didn't say nothin' to him for I was too skeered. De very last time I went to a dance, somepin got atter me and skeered me so my hair riz up 'til I couldn't git my hat on my haid, and dat cyored me of gwine to dances. I ain't never been to no more sich doin's.

"Old Marster was powerful good to his Niggers when dey got sick. He had 'em seed atter soon as it was 'ported to him dat dey was ailin'. Yessum, dere warn't nothin' short 'bout our good Marsters, 'deed dere warn't! Grandpa Stafford had a sore laig and Marse Lordnorth looked atter him and had Uncle Jim dress dat pore old sore laig evvy day. Slaves didn't git sick as often as Niggers does now days. Mammy Mary had all sorts of teas made up for us, 'cordin' to whatever ailment us had. Boneset tea was for colds. De fust thing dey allus done for sore throat was give us tea made of red oak bark wid alum. Scurvy grass tea cleant us out in the springtime, and dey made us wear little sacks of assfiddy (asafetida) 'round our necks to keep off lots of sorts of miseries. Some folkses hung de left hind foot of a mole on a string 'round deir babies necks to make 'em teethe easier. I never done nothin' lak dat to my babies 'cause I never believed in no such foolishment. Some babies is jus' natchelly gwine to teethe easier dan others anyhow.

"I 'members jus' as good as if it was yesterday what Mammy Mary said when she told us de fust news of our freedom. 'You all is free now,' she said. 'You don't none of you belong to Mister Lordnorth nor Mister Alec no more, but I does hope you will all stay on wid 'em, 'cause dey will allus be jus' as good to you as dey has done been in de past."

Me, I warn't even studyin' nothin' 'bout leavin' Marse Alec, but Sarah Ann and Aunt Mary, dey throwed down deir hoes and jus' whooped and hollered 'cause dey was so glad. When dem Yankees come to our place Mammy Mary axed 'em if dey warn't tired of war. 'What does you know 'bout no war?' Dey axed her right back. 'No, us won't never git tired of doin' good.'

Visit

"I stayed on wid my two good Marsters 'til most 3 years atter de war, and den went to wuk for Marse Tye Elder in Crawfordville. Atter dat I wuked for Miss Puss King, and when she left Crawfordville I come on here to Athens and wuked for Miss Tildy Upson on Prince Avenue. Den I went to Atlanta to wuk for Miss Ruth Evage (probably Elliott). Miss Ruth was a niece of Abraham Lincoln's. Her father was President Lincoln's brother and he was a Methodist preacher what lived in Mailpack, New York. I went evvywhar wid Miss Ruth. When me and Miss Ruth was in Philadelphia, I got sick and she sont me home to Athens and I done been here wid my daughter ever since.

Free negroes. Employers 7.

"Lawdy, Miss! I ain't never been married, but I did live wid Major Baker 18 years and us had five chillun. Dey is all daid but two. Niggers didn't pay so much 'tention to gittin' married dem days as dey does now. I stays here wid my gal, Ida Baker. My son lives in Cleveland, Ohio. My fust child was borned when I warn't but 14 years old. De war ended in April and she was borned in November of dat year. Now, Miss! I ain't never told but one white 'oman who her Pa was, so you needn't start axin' me nothin' 'bout dat. She had done been walkin' evvywhar 'fore she died when she was jus' 10 months old and I'm a-tellin' you de truth when I say she had more sense dan a heap of white chillun has when dey is lots older dan she was. Whilst I was off in New York wid Miss Ruth, Major, he up and got married. I reckon he's daid by now. I don't keer nohow, atter de way he done me. I made a good livin' for Major 'til he married again. I seed de 'oman he married once.

"Yes Mam," there was strong emphasis in this reply. "I sho would ruther have slavery days back if I could have my same good Marsters 'cause I never had no hard times den lak I went through atter dey give us freedom. I ain't never got over not bein' able to see Marse Alec no more. I was livin' at Marse Lye Elder's when de gate fell on Marse Alec, and he was crippled and lamed up from dat time on 'til he died. He got to be Governor of Georgia whilst he was crippled. When he got hurt by dat gate, smallpox was evvywhar and dey wouldn't let me go to see 'bout him. Dat most killed me 'cause I did want to go see if dere was somepin' I could do for him.

"Lordy Mussy, Miss! I had a time jinin' up wid de church. I was in Mailpack, New York, wid Miss Ruth when I had de urge to jine up. I told Miss Ruth 'bout it and she said: 'Dere ain't no Baptist church in 10 miles of here.' 'Lord, have mussy!' I said. 'Miss Ruth, what I gwine do? Dese is all Methodist churches up here and I jus' can't jine up wid no Methodists.' 'Yes you can,' she snapped at me, 'cause my own Pa's a-holdin' a 'vival in dis very town and de Methodist church is de best anyhow.' Well, I went on and jined de Reverend Lincoln's Methodist church, but I never felt right 'bout it. Den us went to Philadelphia and soon as I could find a Baptist church dar, I jined up wid it. Northern churches ain't lak our southern churches 'cause de black and white folkses all belong to de same church dar and goes to church together. On dat account I still didn't feel lak I had jined de church. Bless your sweet life, Honey, when I come back to de South, I was quick as I could be to jine up wid a good old southern Baptist church. I sho didn't mean to live outdoors, 'specially atter I dies." Georgia's eyes sparkled and her flow of speech was smooth as she told of her religious experiences. When that subject was exhausted her eyes dimmed again and her speech became less articulate.

Georgia's reeking pipe had been laid aside for the watermelon and not long after that was consumed the restless black fingers sought occupation sewing gay pieces for a quilt. "Miss, I warn't born to be lazy, I warn't raised dat way, and I sho ain't skeered to die.

"Good-bye, Honey," said Georgia, as the interviewer arose and made her way toward the street. "Hurry back and don't forgit to fetch me dat purty pink dress you is a-wearin'. I don't lak white dresses and I ain't never gwine to wear a black one nohow."

....

Georgia was on the back porch washing her face and hands and quarrelling with Ida for not having her breakfast ready at nine-thirty when the interviewer arrived for a re-visit.

"Come in," Georgia invited, "and have a cheer. But, Miss I done told you all I knows 'bout Marse Alec and dem days when I lived on his plantation. You know chillun den warn't 'lowed to hang 'round de grown folks whar dey could hear things what was talked about."

About this time Ida came down from a second-floor kitchen with her mother's breakfast. She was grumbling a little louder on each step of the rickety stairway. "Lord, have mussy! Ma is still a-talkin' 'bout dat old slavery stuff, and it ain't nothin' nohow." After Ida's eyes had rested on the yellow crepe frock just presented Georgia in appreciation of the three hours she had given for the first interview, she became reconciled for the story to be resumed, and even offered her assistance in arousing the recollections of her parent.

"Did I tell you" Georgia began, "dat de man what looked atter Marse Alec's business was his fust cousin? He was de Marse Lordnorth I'se all time talkin' 'bout, and Marse John was Marse Lordnorth's brother. Dere warn't no cook or house gal up at de big house but Ma 'til atter she died, and

Den when Miss Mary Berry tuk charge of de house dey made Uncle Harry and his wife, Aunt 'Liza, house boy and cook.

"Marse Alec growed all his corn on his Googer Crick plantation. He planned for evvything us needed and dere warn't but mighty little dat he didn't have raised to take keer of our needs. Lordy, didn't I tell you what sort of shoes, Polestock shoes is? Dem was de shoes de 'omans wore and dey had extra pieces on de sides so us wouldn't knock holes in 'em too quick.

"De fust time I ever seed Marse Alec to know who he was, I warn't more'n 6 years old. Uncle Stafford had went fishin' and cotched de nicest mess of fish you ever seed. He cleant 'em and put 'em in a pan of water, and told me to take 'em up to de big house to Marse Alec. I was skeered when I went in de big house yard and axed, what looked lak a little boy, whar Marse Alec was, and I was wuss skeered when he said: 'Dis is Marse Alec you is talkin' to. What you want?' I tole him Uncle Stafford sont him de fishes and he told me: 'Take 'em to de kitchen and tell 'Liza to cook 'em for me.' I sho ain't never gwine to forgit dat.

"One day dey sont me wid a bucket of water to de field, and I had to go through de peach orchard. I et so many peaches, I was 'most daid when I got back to de house. Dey had to drench me down wid sweet milk, and from dat day to dis I ain't never laked peaches. From den on Marse Alec called me de 'peach gal.'

"Marse Alec warn't home much of de time, but when he was dar he used to walk down to de cabins and laugh and talk to his Niggers. He used to sing a song for de slave chillun dat run somepin lak dis:

'Walk light ladies
De cake's all dough,
You needn't mind de
weather,
If de wind don't blow.'

Georgia giggled when she came to the end of the stanza. "Us didn't know when he was a-singin' dat tune to us chillun dat when us growed up us would be cake walkin' to de same song.

"On Sundays, whenever Marse Alec was home, he done lots of readin' out of a great big old book. I didn't know what it was, but he was pow'ful busy wid it. He never had no parties or dancin' dat I knows 'bout, but he was all time havin' dem big 'portant mens at his house talkin' 'bout de business what tuk him off from home so much. I used to see Lawyer Toombs dere heaps of times. He was a big, fine lookin' man. Another big lawyer was all time comin' dar too, but I done lost his name. Marse Alec had so awful much sense in his haid dat folkses said it stunted his growin'. Anyhow, long as he lived he warn't no bigger dan a boy.

"When Uncle Harry's and Aunt 'Liza's daughter what was named 'Liza, got married he was in Washin'ton or some place lak dat. He writ word to Marse Linton, his half-brother, to pervide a weddin' for her. I knows 'bout dat 'cause I et some of dat barbecue. Dat's all I 'members 'bout her weddin'. I done forgot de name of de bridegroom. He lived on some other plantation. Aunt 'Liza had two gals and one boy. He was named Allen.

"Whilst Marse Alec was President or somepin, he got sick and had to come back home, and it warn't long atter dat 'fore de surrender. Allen was 'pinted to watch for de blue coats. When dey come to take Marse Alec off, dey was all over the place wid deir guns. Us Niggers hollered and cried and tuk on pow'ful 'cause us sho thought dey was gwine to kill him on account of his bein' such a high up man on de side what dey was fightin'. All de Niggers followed 'em to de depot when dey tuk Marse Alec and Uncle Pierce away. Dey kept Marse Alec in prison off somewhar a long time but dey sont Pierce back home 'fore long.

"I seed Jeff Davis when dey brung him through Crawfordville on de train. Dey had him all fastened up wid chains. Dey told me dat a Nigger 'oman put pizen in Jeff Davis' somepin t'eat and dat was what kilt him. One thing sho, our Marse Alec warn't pizened by nobody. He was comin' from de field one day when a big old heavy gate fell down on him, and even if he did live a long time atterwards dat was what was de cause of his death.

"I seed Uncle Pierce 'fore he died and us sot and talked and cried 'bout Marse Alec. Yessum, us sho did have de best Marster in de world. If ever a man went to Heaven, Marse Alec did. I sho does wish our good old Marster was livin' now. Now, Miss, I done told you all I can ricollec' 'bout dem days. I thanks you a lot for dat purty yaller dress, and I hopes you comes back to see me again sometime."

*
***
***
*

100192

ALICE BATTLE, EX-SLAVE

HAWKINSVILLE, GEORGIA

(INTERVIEWED BY ELIZABETH WATSON- 1936)

During the 1840's, Emanuel Caldwell--born in North Carolina, and Neal Anne Caldwell--born in South Carolina, were brought to Macon by "speculators" and sold to Mr. Ed Marshal of Bibb County. Some time thereafter, this couple married on Mr. Marshal's plantation, and their second child, born about 1850, was Alice Battle.

From her birth until freedom, Alice was a chattel of this Mr. Marshal, whom she refers to as a humane man, though inclined to use the whip when occasion demanded.

Followed to its conclusion, Alice's life history is void of thrills and simply an average ex-slave's story. As a slave, she was well fed, well clothed, and well treated, as were her brother and sister slaves. Her mother was a weaver, her father --a field hand, and she did both housework and plantation labor.

Alice saw the Yankee pass her ex-master's home with their famous prisoner, Jeff Davis, after his capture, in '65. The Yankee band, says she, was playing "We'll hang Jeff Davis on a Sour Apple Tree". Some of the soldiers "took time out" to rob the Marshal smokehouse. The Whites and Negroes were all badly frightened, but the "damyankees didn't harm nobody".

After freedom, Alice remained with the Marshals until Christmas, when she moved away. Later, she and her family moved back to the Marshal plantation for a few years. A few years still later, Alice married a Battle "Nigger".

Since the early '70's, Alice has "drifted around" quite a bit. She and her husband are now too old and feeble to work. They live with one of their sons, and are objects of charity.

PLANTATION LIFE

JASPER BATTLE
112 Berry St.,
Athens, Ga.

Written by: Grace McCune (white)
Athens -

Edited by: Sarah H. Hall
Athens -

Leila Harris
Augusta -
and
John N. Booth
District Supervisor
Federal Writers' Project
Residencies 6 & 7.

JASPER BATTLE
Ex-Slave - Age 80.

The shade of the large water oaks in Jasper's yard was a welcome sight when the interviewer completed the long walk to the old Negro's place in the sweltering heat of a sunny July afternoon. The old house appeared to be in good condition and the yard was clean and tidy. Jasper's wife, Lula, came around the side of the house in answer to the call for Jasper. A large checked apron almost covered her blue dress and a clean white headcloth concealed her hair. Despite her advanced age, she seemed to be quite spry.

"Jus' come back here whar I'se a-doin' de white folks' washin'," she said. "Jasper's done been powerful sick and I can't leave him by hisself none. I brung him out here in de shade so I could watch him and 'tend to him whilst I wuks. Jasper stepped on a old plank what had two rusty nails in it, and both of 'em went up in his foot a fur ways. I done driv dem nails plumb up to dey haids in de north side of a tree and put jimpson weed poultices on Jasper's foot, but it's still powerful bad off."

By this time we had arrived within sight and earshot of the old rocking chair where Jasper sat with his foot propped high in another chair. His chair had long ago been deprived of its rockers. The injured member appeared to be swollen and was covered with several layers of the jimpson weed leaves. The old man's thin form was clothed in a faded blue shirt and old gray cotton trousers. His clothes were clean and his white hair was in marked contrast to his shining but wrinkled black face. He smiled when Lula explained the nature of the proposed interview. "'Scuse me, Missy," he apologized, "for not gittin' up, 'cause I jus' can't use dis old foot much, but you jus' have a seat here in de shade and rest yourself." Lula now excused herself, saying: "I jus' got to hurry and git de white folks' clothes washed and dried 'fore it rains," and she resumed her work in the shade of another huge tree where a fire was burning brightly under her washpot and a row of sud-filled tubs occupied a long bench.

"Lula, she has to wuk all de time," Jasper explained, "and she don't never have time to listen to me talk. I'se powerful glad somebody is willin' to stop long enough to pay some heed whilst I talks 'bout somepin. Dem days 'fore de war was good old days, 'specially for de colored folks. I know, 'cause my Mammy done told me so. You see I was mighty little and young when de war was over, but I heared de old folks do lots of talkin' 'bout dem times whilst I was a-growin' up, and den too, I stayed right dar on dat same place 'til I was 'bout grown. It was Marse Henry Jones' plantation 'way off down in Taliaferro County, nigh Crawfordville, Georgy. Mammy b'longed to Marse Henry. She was Harriet Jones. Daddy was Simon Battle and his owner was Marse Billie Battle. De Battle's plantation was off down dar nigh de Jones' place. When my Mammy and Daddy got married Marse

Henry wouldn't sell Mammy, and Marse Billie wouldn't sell Daddy, so dey didn't git to see one another but twice a week - dat was on Wednesday and Sadday nights - 'til atter de war was done over. I kin still 'member Daddy comin' over to Marse Henry's plantation to see us.

"Marse Henry kept a lot of slaves to wuk his big old plantation whar he growed jus' evvything us needed to eat and wear 'cept sugar and coffee and de brass toes for our home-made, brogan shoes. Dere allus was a-plenty t'eat and wear on dat place.

"Slave quarters was log cabins built in long rows. Some had chimblies in de middle, twixt two rooms, but de most of 'em was jus' one-room cabins wid a stick and mud chimbly at de end. Dem chimblies was awful bad 'bout ketchin' on fire. Didn't nobody have no glass windows. Dey jus' had plain plank shutters for blinds and de doors was made de same way, out of rough planks. All de beds was home-made and de best of 'em was corded. Dey made holes in de sides and foots and haidpieces, and run heavy home-made cords in dem holes. Dey wove 'em crossways in and out of dem holes from one side to another 'til dey had 'em ready to lay de mattress mat on. I'se helped to pull dem cords tight many a time. Our mattress ticks was made of homespun cloth and was stuffed wid wheat straw. 'Fore de mattress tick was put on de bed a stiff mat wove out of white oak splits was laid on top of de cords to pertect de mattress and make it lay smooth. Us was 'lowed to pick up all de old dirty cotton 'round de place to make our pillows out of.

"Jus' a few of de slave famblies was 'lowed to do deir own cookin' 'cause Marster kept cooks up at de big house what never had nothin' else to do but cook for de white folks and slaves. De big old fireplace in dat kitchen at de big house was more dan eight feet wide and you could pile whole sticks of cord-wood on it. It had racks acrost to hang de pots on and big ovens and little ovens and big, thick, iron fryin' pans wid long handles and hefty iron lids. Dey could cook for a hunderd people at one time in dat big old kitchen easy. At one time dere was tables acrost one end of de kitchen for de slaves t'eat at, and de slave chillun et dar too.

"Marster was mighty good to slave chillun. He never sont us out to wuk in de fields 'til us was 'most growed-up, say 12 or 14 years old. A Nigger 12 or 14 years old dem days was big as a white child 17 or 18 years old. Why Miss, Niggers growed so fast, dat most of de Nigger nurses warn't no older dan de white chillun dey tuk keer of. Marster said he warn't gwine to send no babies to de fields. When slave chillun got to be 'bout 9 or 10 years old dey started 'em to fetchin' in wood and water, cleanin' de yards, and drivin' up de cows at night. De bigges' boys was 'lowed to measure out and fix de stock feed, but de most of us chillun jus' played in de cricks and woods all de time. Sometimes us played Injuns and made so much fuss dat old Aunt Nancy would come out to de woods to see what was wrong, and den when she found us was jus' a-havin' fun, she stropped us good for skeerin' her.

"Mammy's job was to make all de cloth. Dat was what she done all de time; jus' wove cloth. Some of de others cyarded de bats and spun thread, but Mammy, she jus' wove on so reg'lar dat she made enough cloth for clothes for all dem slaves on de plantation and, it's a fact, us did have plenty of clothes. All de nigger babies wore dresses made jus' alak for boys and gals. I was sho'ly mighty glad when dey 'lowed me to git rid of dem dresses and wear shirts. I was 'bout 5 years old den, but dat boys' shirt made me feel powerful mannish. Slave gals wore homespun cotton dresses, and dey had plenty of dem dresses, so as dey could keep nice and clean all de time. Dey knitted all de socks and stockin's for winter. Dem gals wore shawls, and dere poke bonnets had ruffles 'round 'em. All de shoes was home-made too. Marster kept one man on de plantation what didn't do nothin' but make shoes. Lordy, Missy! What would gals say now if dey had to wear dem kind of clothes? Dey would raise de roof plumb offen de house. But jus' let me tell you, a purty young gal dressed in dem sort of clothes would look mighty sweet to me right now.

"Us never could eat all de meat in Marster's big old smokehouse. Sometimes he tuk hams to de store and traded 'em for sugar and coffee. Plenty of 'bacco was raised on dat plantation for all de white folks and de growed-up Niggers. Slave chillun warn't sposen to have none, so us had to swipe what 'bacco us got. If our Mammies found out 'bout us gittin' 'bacco, dey stropped us 'til de skin was most off our backs, but sometimes us got away wid a little. If us seed any of de old folks was watchin' us, us slipped de 'bacco from one to another of us whilst dey s'arched us, and it went mighty bad on us if dey found it.

"Slaves went to de white folks' church and listened to de white preachers. Dere warn't no colored preacher 'lowed to preach in dem churches den. Dey preached to de white folks fust and den dey let de colored folks come inside and hear some preachin' atter dey was through wid de white folks. But on de big 'vival meetin' days dey 'lowed de Niggers to come in and set in de gallery and listen at de same time dey preached to de white folks. When de sermon was over dey had a big dinner spread out on de grounds and dey had jus' evvything good t'eat lak chickens, barbecued hogs and lambs, pies, and lots of watermelons. Us kept de watermelons in de crick 'til dey was ready to cut 'em. A white gentleman, what dey called Mr. Kilpatrick, done most of de preachin'. He was from de White Plains neighborhood. He sho' did try mighty hard to git evvybody to 'bey de Good Lord and keep his commandments.

"Mr. Kilpatrick preached all de funerals too. It 'pears lak a heap more folks is a-dyin' out dese days dan died den, and folks was a heap better den to folks in trouble. Dey would go miles and miles den when dey didn't have no auto'biles, to help folks what was in trouble. Now, dey won't go next door when dere's death in de house. Den, when anybody died de fust thing dey done was to shroud 'em and lay 'em out on de coolin' board 'til Old Marster's cyarpenter could git de coffin made up. Dere warn't no embalmers dem days and us had to bury folks de next day atter dey died. De coffins was jus' de same for white folks and deir slaves. On evvy plantation dere was a piece of ground fenced in for a graveyard whar dey buried white folks and slaves too. My old Daddy is buried down yonder on Marse Henry's plantation right now.

"When a slave wanted to git married up wid a gal, he didn't ax de gal, but he went and told Marster 'bout it. Marster would talk to de gal and if she was willin', den Marster would tell all de other Niggers us was a-goin' to have a weddin'. Dey would all come up to de big house and Marster would tell de couple to jine hands and jump backwards over a broomstick, and den he pernounced 'em man and wife. Dey didn't have to have no licenses or nothin' lak dey does now. If a man married up wid somebody on another place, he had to git a pass from his Marster, so as he could go see his wife evvy Wednesday and Sadday nights. When de patterollers cotched slaves out widout no passes, dey evermore did beat 'em up. Leastways dat's what Mammy told me.

"Durin' de big war all de white folkses was off a-fightin' 'cept dem what was too old to fight or what was too bad crippled and 'flicted. Dey stayed home and looked atter de 'omans and chillun. Somebody sont Mist'ess word dat dem yankees was on de way to our plantation and she hid evvything she could, den had de hogs and hosses driv off to de swamps and hid. Mammy was crazy 'bout a pet pig what Marster had done give her, so Mist'ess told her to go on down to dat swamp quick, and hide dat little pig. Jus' as she was a-runnin' back in de yard, dem yankees rid in and she seed 'em a-laughin' fit to kill. She looked 'round to see what dey was tickled 'bout and dere followin' her lak a baby was dat pig. Dem yankees was perlite lak, and dey never bothered nothin' on our place, but dey jus' plumb ruint evvything on some of de plantations right close to our'n. Dey tuk nigh evvything some of our neighbors had t'eat, most all deir good hosses, and anything else dey wanted. Us never did know why dey never bothered our white folkses' things.

"When dey give us our freedom us went right on over to Marse Billie Battle's place and stayed dar wid Daddy 'bout a year; den Daddy come wid us back to Marse Henry's, and dar us stayed 'til Old Marster died. Long as he lived atter de war, he wukked most of his help on sheers, and seed dat us was tuk keer of jus' lak he had done when us all b'longed to him. Us never went to school much 'cause Mammy said white folks didn't lak for Niggers to have no larnin', but atter de war was done over our Old Mist'ess let colored chillun have some lessons in a little cabin what was built in de back yard for de white chillun to go to school in.

"Atter dey buried our Old Marster, us moved down to Hancock County and farmed dar, 'cause dat was all us knowed how to do. Us got together and raised money to buy ground enough for a churchyard and a graveyard for colored folks. Dat graveyard filled up so fast dat dey had to buy more land several times. Us holped 'em build de fust colored church in Hancock County.

"School for colored chillun was held den in our church house. Our teacher was a white man, Mr. Tom Andrews, and he was a mighty good teacher, but Lordy, how strick he was! Dese here chillun don't know nothin' 'bout school. Us went early in de mornin', tuk our dinner in a bucket, and never left 'til four o' clock, and sometimes dat was 'most nigh sundown. All day us studied dat blue back speller, and dat white teacher of ours sho' tuk de skin offen our backs if us didn't mind him. Dere warn't no fussin' and fightin' and foolin' 'round on de way home, 'cause dat white teacher 'lowed he had control of us 'til us got to our Mammies' doors and if us didn't git for home in a hurry, it was jus' too bad for us when he tuk it out on us next day wid dat long hick'ry switch.

"Things is sho' diffunt now. Folks ain't good now as dey was den, but dere is gwine to be a change. I may not be here to see it, but it's a-comin' 'cause de Good Lord is done 'sied (prophesied) it, and it's got to be. God's sayin' is comin' to pass jus' as sho' as us is livin' and settin' in de shade of dis here tree.

"Lordy, Miss! How come you axes 'bout colored folks'es weddin's? I was a-courtin' a little 14-year old gal named Lovie Williams, but her Mammy runned me off and said she warn't gwine to let Lovie git married up wid nobody 'til she got big enough. I jus' bought dem licenses and watched for my chanct and den I stole dat gal right from under her Mammy's eyes. My Mammy knowed all 'bout it and holped us git away. Us didn't have no time for no weddin'. De best us could do was jus' to git ourselfs married up. Lovie's Mammy raised de Old Ned, but us didn't keer den, 'cause it was too late for her to do nothin' to part us. Lovie was one of the bestest gals what ever lived. Us raised 12 chillun and I never had one speck of trouble wid her. Lovie's done been daid 15 years now."

His voice trembled as he talked about his first wife, and Lula almost stopped her work to listen. This kind of talk did not please her and her expression grew stern. "You done talked a-plenty," she told him. "You ain't strong 'nough to do no more talkin'," but Jasper was not willing to be silenced. "I reckon I knows when I'se tired. I ain't gwine to hush 'til I gits good and ready," was his protest. "Yes Missy," he continued. "All our chillun is done daid now 'cept four and dey is 'way off up North. Ain't nobody left here 'cept me and Lula. Lula is pow'ful good to me. I done got too old to wuk, and can't do nothin' nohow wid dis old foot so bad off. I'se ready and even anxious to go when de Good Lord calls for old Jasper to come to de Heav'nly Home.

"I ain't heared nothin' from my only brother in over 7 years. I 'spose he still lives in Crawfordville. Missy, I wishes I could go back down to Crawfordville one more time. I kin jus' see our old homeplace on de plantation down dar now. Lula a-washin' here, makes me study 'bout de old washplace on Marse Henry's plantation. Dere was a long bench full of old wood tubs, and a great big iron pot for bilin' de clothes, and de batten block and stick. Chillun beat de clothes wid de batten stick and kept up de fire 'round de pot whilst de 'omans leaned over de tubs washin' and a-singin' dem old songs. You could hear 'em 'most a mile away. Now and den one of de 'omans would stop singin' long enough to yell at de chillun to 'git more wood on dat fire 'fore I lash de skin offen your back.'

"Oh Missy, dem was good old days. Us would be lucky to have 'em back again, 'specially when harvest time comes 'round. You could hear Niggers a-singin' in de fields 'cause dey didn't have no worries lak dey got now. When us got de corn up from de fields, Niggers come from far and nigh to Marster's corn-shuckin'. Dat cornshuckin' wuk was easy wid evvybody singin' and havin' a good time together whilst dey made dem shucks fly. De corn-shuckin' captain led all de singin' and he set right up on top of de highes' pile of corn. De chillun was kept busy a-passin' de liquor jug 'round. Atter it started gittin' dark, Marster had big bonfires built up and plenty of torches set 'round so as dere would be plenty of light. Atter dey et all dey wanted of dem good things what had done been cooked up for de big supper, den de wrastlin' matches started, and Marster allus give prizes to de best wrastlers. Dere warn't no fussin' and fightin' 'lowed on our place, and dem wrastlin' matches was all in good humor and was kept orderly. Marster wanted evvybody to be friends on our plantation and to stay dat way, for says he: 'De Blessed Saviour done said for us to love our neighbor as ourselfs, and to give and what us gives is gwine to come back to us.' Missy, de Good Lord's word is always right."

The interviewer was preparing to leave when one of Jasper's old friends approached the sheltering tree in the yard, where the interview was drawing to a close. "Brudder Paul," said Jasper, "I wisht you had come sooner 'cause Missy, here, and me is done had de bestes' time a-goin' back over dem old times when folks loved one another better dan dey does now. Good-bye Missy, you done been mighty kind and patient wid old Jasper. Come back again some time."

. . . . .

EXTRAS:
F.S.T.-Lost Dist. ofc.

Ex. SIV- #10.

100183

72

ARRIE BINNS of WASHINGTON-WILKES

by

Minnie Branham Stonestreet
Washington-Wilkes
Georgia

ARRIE BINNS of WASHINGTON-WILKES

Arrie Binns lives in Baltimore, a negro suburb of Washington-Wilkes, in a little old tumbled down kind of a cottage that used to be one of the neatest and best houses of the settlement and where she has lived for the past sixty-odd years. In the yard of her home is one of the most beautiful holly trees to be found anywhere. She set it there herself over fifty years ago. She recalled how her friends predicted bad luck would befall her because she "sot out er holly", but not being in the least bit superstitious she paid them "no mind" and has enjoyed her beautiful tree all these years. Many lovely oaks are around her house; she set them there long ago when she was young and with her husband moved into their new home and wanted to make it as attractive as possible. She is all alone now. Her husband died some years ago and three of her four children have passed on. Her "preacher son" who was her delight, died not very long ago. All this sorrow has left Aunt Arrie old and sad; her face is no longer lighted by the smile it used to know. She is a tiny little scrap of a woman with the softest voice and is as neat as can be. She wears an oldfashioned apron all the time and in cool weather there is always a little black cape around her frail shoulders and held together with a plain old gold "breastpin".

She was born in Lincoln County (Georgia), her mother was Emeline Sybert and her father Jordan Sybert. They belonged to Mr. Jones Sybert and his wife "Miss Peggy". After freedom they changed their surname to Gullatt as they liked that better. Arrie was among the oldest of nine children. The night she was born the stork brought a little baby girl to the home of a white family just across the creek from the Syberts. The little white girl was named Arine so "Miss Peggy" named the little new black baby girl Arrie, and that is how it happened she was given such an odd name.

Arrie said she was "15 er 16 years old when the war broke (1865), I wuz big enough to be lookin' at boys an' dey lookin' at me." She remembers the days of war, how when the battle of Atlanta was raging they heard the distant rumble of cannon, and how "upsot" they all were. Her master died of "the consumption" during the war. She recalls how hard it was after his death. The Syberts had no children and there was no one to turn to after his death. Arrie tells of her Master's illness, how she was the housemaid and was called upon to fan him and how she would get so tired and sleepy she would nod a little, the fan dropping from hands into his face. He would take it up and "crack my haid with the handle to wake me up. I wuz allus so sorry when I done that, but I jest had ter nod."

She told about how bad the overseers were and the trouble they gave until finally "old Miss turned off ther one she had an' put my Pa in his place to manage things and look after the work." Arrie was never punished, (not any more than having her head cracked by her Master when she nodded while fanning him.) "No mam, not none of our niggers wuz whipped. Why I recollect once, my brother wuz out without a pass an' de patter rollers kotch him and brung him to old Miss and said he'd have ter be whipped, old Miss got so mad she didn't know what ter do, she said nobody wuz a goin' ter whip her niggers, but the patter roller men 'sisted so she said after er while, 'Well, but I'm goin' ter stan' right here an' when I say stop, yer got ter stop', an' they 'greed to dat, an' the third time dey hit him she raised her han' an' said 'STOP' an' dey had ter let my brother go. My Miss wuz a big 'oman, she'd weigh nigh on ter three hundred pound, I 'spect."

After her master's death Arrie had to go into the field to work. She recalled with a little chuckle, the old cream horse, "Toby" she use to plow. She loved Toby, she said, and they did good work. When not plowing she said she "picked er round in the fields" doing whatever she could. She and the other slaves were not required to do very hard work. Her mother was a field hand, but in the evenings she spun and wove down in their cabin. Aunt Arrie added "an' I did love to hear that old spinnin' wheel. It made a low kind of a whirring sound that made me sleepy." She said her mother, with all the other negro women on the place, had "a task of spinnin' a spool at night", and they spun and wove on rainy days too. "Ma made our clothes an' we had pretty dresses too. She dyed some blue and brown striped. We growed the indigo she used fer the blue, right dar on the plantation, and she used bark and leaves to make the tan and brown colors."

Aunt Arrie said the Doctor was always called in when they

were sick, "but we never sont fer him lesse'n somebody wuz real sick. De old folks doctored us jest fer little ailments. Dey give us lye tea fer colds. (This was made by taking a few clean ashes from the fire place, putting them in a little thin bag and pouring boiling water over them and let set for a few minutes. This had to be given very weak or else it would be harmful, Aunt Arrie explained.) Garlic and whiskey, and den, dar ain't nothin' better fer the pneumony dan splinter tea, I've cured bad cases with it." (That is made by pouring boiling water over lightwood splinters.)

Aunt Arrie told of their life on the plantation and it was not unlike that of other slaves who had good masters who looked after them. They had plenty to eat and to wear, Their food was given them and they cooked and ate their meals in the cabins in family groups. Santa Claus always found his way to the Quarters and brought them stick candy and other things to eat. She said for their Christmas dinner there was always a big fat hen and a hog head.

In slavery days the negroes had quiltings, dances, picnics and everybody had a good time, Aunt Arrie said, "an' I kin dance yit when I hears a fiddle'." They had their work to do in the week days, but when Sundays came there was no work, everybody rested and on "preachin' days" went to Church. Her father took them all to old Rehoboth, the neighborhood white church, and they worshiped together, white and black, the negroes in the gallery. That was back in the days when there was "no lookin' neither to the right nor to the left" when in church; no matter what happened, no one could even half way smile. This all was much harder than having to listen to the long tiresome sermons of those days, Arrie thinks, specially when she recalled on one occasion "when Mr. Sutton wuz a preachin' a old goat got up under the Church an' every time Mr. Sutton would say something out real loud that old goat would go 'Bah-a-a Bah ba-a-a' an' we couldn't laugh a bit. I most busted, I wanted ter laugh so bad."

"Yassum, in dem days" continued Aunt Arrie, "all us colored folks went to the white folks church kase us didn't have no churches of our own and day want no colored preachers den, but some what wuz called "Chairbacks". The Chairback fellows went er round preachin' an' singin' in the cabins down in the Quarters and dey use ter have the bes' meetin's, folks would be converted an' change dey way. De hymns dey sung de most wuz "Amazin' Grace" an' "Am I Born ter Die?" I 'members de meetin's us use ter have down in our cabin an' how everybody would pray an' sing."

"Dey ain't nothin' lak it use ter be," sighed Aunt Arrie, "Now when I first could recollect, when a nigger died they sot up with de corpse all night and de next day had de funeral an' when dey started to the burial ground with the body every body in the whole procession would sing hymns. I've heard 'em 'nough times clear 'cross the fields, singin' and moanin' as they went. Dem days of real feelin' an' keerin' is gone."

When freedom came there were sad times on the Sybert plantation, Arrie said. "Old Miss cried and cried, and all us cried too. Old Miss said "You'al jest goin' off to perish." Aunt Jennie, one of the oldest women slaves stayed on with her and took keer of her, but all us stayed on a while. Us didn't know whar to go an' what ter do, an' den come Dr. Peters and Mr. Allen frum Arkansas to git han's to go out dar an' work fer dem. My Pa took his family and we stayed two years. It took us might nigh ar whole week to git dar, we went part way on de train and den rid de steam boat up de Mississippi River ter de landin'. We worked in the cotton field out dar and done all kinds er work on de farm, but us didn't like an' Dr. Peters an' Mr. Allen give my Pa money fer us ter come home on. 'Fore we could git started my oldest brother wanted to come home so bad he jest pitched out and walked all de way frum Arkansas to our old home in Georgy. We come back by Memphis and den come on home on de train. [When we wuz out dar I went to school an' got as far as 'Baker'. Dat's de only schoolin' I ever had."]

Aunt Arrie told about her courtship and marriage, she remembers all about it and grew rather sentimental and sad while she talked. She said that Franklin Binns was going with her before she went to live in Arkansas and when she came home he picked up the courtship where he had left off when she went away. He would ride 20 miles on horseback to see her. He brought her candy and nice things to eat, but she still wouldn't "give him no satisfaction 'bout whether she keered fer him er not." She said other men wanted to come to see her, but she paid them not one bit of attention. "No mam, I wouldn't 'cept of them, I never did go with in an' everybody, I don't do dat yit." She said one day Franklin was to see her and said "Less us marry, I think 'nough of you to marry." She said she wouldn't tell him nothin' so he went to see her parents and they agreed, so she married him sometime later. They were married by a white minister, Mr. Joe Carter.

Aunt Arrie leads a lonely life now, She grieves for her loved ones more than negroes usually do. She doesn't get about much, but "I does go over to see Sis Lou (a neighbor) every now an' den fer consolation." She says she is living on borrowed time because she has always taken care of herself and worked and been honest. She said that now she is almost at the close of her life waiting day by day for the call to come, she is glad she knew slavery, glad she was reared by good white people who taught her the right way to live, and she added: "Mistess, I'se so glad I allus worked hard an' been honest - hit has sho paid me time an' time agin."

Dist. 5. Driskell, (LKH) EX S1V. # 7.

100047

~~SLAVERY AS SEEN BY~~ HENRY BLAND - EX-SLAVE

Henry Bland is one of the few living ex-slaves who was born on a plantation near Edenton, Ga., in 1851. His parents were Martha and Sam Coxton. In this family group were three other children, two girls and one boy, who was the oldest. When questioned regarding the birthplace and the movements of his parents, Mr. Bland stated that his father was born in Hancock County, Ga. His mother along with her mother was brought to Georgia by the speculator with a drove of other slaves. The first thing that he remembers of his parents is when he was quite small and was allowed to remain in the master's kitchen in the "big house" where his mother was cook.

Mr. Coxton, who was the owner of Mr. Bland and his family, was described as being a very rich and influential man in the community where he lived. Says Mr. Bland, "His only fault was that of drinking too much of the whisky that he distilled on the plantation." Unlike some of the other slave owners in that section, Mr. Coxton was very kind to his slaves. His plantation was a large one and on it was raised cotton, corn, cane, vegetables, and live stock. More cotton was grown than anything else.

From the time he was 1 year and 6 months of age until he was 9 years old he lived in the "big house" with his mother. At night he slept on the floor there. In spite of this, his and his mother's treatment was considerably better than that received by those slaves who worked in the fields. While their food consisted of the same things as did that of the field slaves, sometimes choice morsels came back to the kitchen from the master's table. He says that his mother's clothes were of better quality than the other slave women (those who were not employed in the house).

As a child his first job was to cut wood for the stove, pick up chips, and to drive the cows to and from the pasture. When 9 years old he was sent to the field as a plow boy. Here he worked with a large number of other slaves (he does not know the exact number) who were divided into two groups, the plow group and the hoe group. His father happened to be the foreman of the hoe gang. His brothers and sisters also worked here in the fields being required to hoe as well as plow. When picking time came, everyone was required to pick. The usual amount of cotton each person was required to pick was 200 lbs. per day. However, when this amount was not picked by some they were not punished by the overseer, as was the case on neighboring plantations, because Mr. Coxton realized that some could do more work than others. Mr. Coxton often told his overseer that he had not been hired to whip the slaves, but to teach them how to work.

Says Mr. Bland: "Our working hours were the same as on any other plantation. We had to get up every morning before sun-up and when it was good and light we were in the field. A bugle was blown to wake us." All the slaves stayed in the field until dark. After leaving the field they were never required to do any work but could spend their time as they saw fit to. No work was required on Saturday or Sunday with the exception that the stock had to be cared for. Besides these days when no work was required, there was the 4th of July and Christmas on which the slaves were permitted to do as they pleased. These two latter dates were usually spent in true holiday spirit as the master usually gave a big feast in the form of a barbecue and allowed them to invite their friends.

When darkness came they sang and danced and this was what they called a "frolic." As a general rule this same thing was permitted after the crops had been gathered. Music for these occasions was furnished by violin, banjo and a clapping of hands. Mr. Bland says that he used to help furnish this music as Mr. Coxton had bought him a violin.

On the Coxton plantation all slaves always had a sufficient amount of clothing. These clothes which were issued when needed and not at any certain time included articles for Sunday wear as well as articles for work. Those servants who worked in the "big house" wore practically the same clothes as the master and his wife with the possible exception that it met the qualification of being second-handed. An issue of work clothing included a heavy pair of work shoes called brogans, homespun shirts and a pair of jeans pants. A pair of knitted socks was also included

The women wore homespun dresses for their working clothes. For Sunday wear the men were given white cotton shirts and the women white cotton dresses. All clothing was made on the plantation by those women who were too old for field work.

In the same manner that clothing was sufficient, so was food plentiful. At the end of each week each family was given 4 lbs. of meat, 1 peck of meal, and some syrup. Each person in a family was allowed to raise a garden and so they had vegetables whenever they wished to. In addition to this they were allowed to raise chickens, to hunt and to fish. However, none of the food that was secured in any of the ways mentioned above could be sold. When anyone wished to hunt, Mr. Cexton supplied the gun and the shot.

Although the slaves cooked for themselves, their breakfast and dinner were usually sent to them in the fields after it had been prepared in the cook house. The reason for this was that they had to get up too soon in the morning, and at noon too much time would be lost if they were permitted to go to their cabins for lunch.

The children who were too young to work in the field were cared for by some old slave who likewise was unable to do field work. The children were usually fed pot liquor, corn bread, milk, syrup, and vegetables. Each one had his individual cup to eat from. The food on Sunday was usually no different from that of any other day of the week. However, Mr. Bland says that they never had to break in the smokehouse because of hunger.

When asked to describe the living quarters of the slaves on his plantation he looked around his room and muttered: "Dey wuz a lot better than dis one." Some of the cabins were made of logs and some of weatherboards. The chinks in the walls were sealed with mud. In some instances boards were used on the inside to keep the weather out. There were usually two windows, shutters being used in the place of window panes. The chimney and fireplace were made of mud and stones. All cooking was done at the fireplace as none of them were provided with stoves. Iron cooking utensils were used. To boil food a pot was hung over the fire by means of a hook.

The remaining furniture was a bench which served as a chair, and a crude bed. Rope running from side to side served as bed springs. The mattress was made of straw or hay. For lighting purposes, pine knots and candles were used. The slaves on the Coxton plantation were also fortunate in that all cabins had wood floors. All cabins and their furnishings were built by the slaves who learned the use of hammer and saw from white artisans whom Mr. Coxton employed from time to time. Mr. Bland remarked that his father was a blacksmith, having learned the trade in this manner.

A doctor was employed regularly by Mr. Coxton to minister to the needs of the slaves in time of illness. "We also had our own medicine," says Mr. Bland. At different times excursions were made to the woods where "yarbs" (herbs) were gathered. Various kinds of teas and medicines were made by boiling these roots in water. The usual causes of illness on this plantation were colds, fevers, and constipation. Castor oil and salts were also used to a great extent. If an individual was too ill to work an older slave had to nurse this person.

No effort was made by Mr. Coxton to teach his slaves anything except manual training. A slave who could use his hands at skilled work was more valuable than the ordinary field hand. If, however, a slave secured a book, Mr. Coxton would help him learn to read it. Above all, religious training was not denied. As a matter of fact, Mr. Coxton required each one of his servants to dress in his Sunday clothes and to go to church every Sunday. Services for all were held at the white church - the slaves sitting on one side and the masters on the other. All preaching was done by a white pastor.

No promiscuous relationships were allowed. If a man wanted to marry he merely pointed out the woman of his choice to the master. He in turn called her and told her that such and such an individual wished her for a wife. If she agreed they were pronounced man and wife and were permitted to live together.

Henry Bland, ex-slave.

The slaves on his plantation were great believers in roots and their values in the use of conjuring people.

Mr. Bland doesn't remember ever seeing anyone sold by Mr. Coxton, but he heard that on other nearby plantations slaves were placed on an auction block and sold like cattle.

None of the slaves were ever whipped or beaten by Mr. Coxton or by anyone else. If a rule was broken the offender was called before Mr. Coxton where he was talked to. In some cases a whipping was promised and that ended the matter. The "Paddie Rollers" whipped the slaves from other plantations when they were caught off of their premises without a "pass" but this was never the case when a slave belonging to Mr. Coxton broke this rule. Mr. Bland remembers that once he and some of his fellow slaves were away from home without a pass when they were seen by the "Paddie Rollers" who started after them. When they were recognized as belonging to Mr. Coxton one of them (Paddie Rollers) said: "Don't bother them; that's them d---'("free niggers'." The Paddie Rollers were not allowed to come on the Coxton plantation to whip his slaves or any other owner's slaves who happened to be visiting at the time. Mr. Coxton required that they all be on the plantation by nightfall.

(The above seems to be rather conclusive proof of Mr. Coxton's influence in the community.)

Whenever a slave committed a crime against the State, his master usually had to pay for the damage done or pay the slave's fine. It was then up to him to see that the offender was punished.

Mr. Coxton once saw him (Mr. Bland) beat another slave(who was a guest at a frolic) when this visitor attempted to draw a pistol on him. Mr. Bland was upheld in his action and told by Mr. Coxton that he had better always fight back when anyone struck him, whether the person was white or black. Further, if he (Mr. Coxton) heard of his not fighting back a whipping would be in store for him.

Mr. Coxton was different from some of the slave owners in that he gave the head of each family spending money at Christmas time - the amount varying with the size of the family.

"When the Civil War was begun the master seemed to be worried all the time" states Mr. Bland. "He was afraid that we would be freed and then he would have to hire us to do his work."

When asked to describe his feelings about the war and the possibility of his being freed, Mr. Bland said that he had no particular feeling of gladness at all. The outcome of the war did not interest him at all because Mr. Coxton was such a good master he didn't care whether he was freed or not. His fellow slaves felt the same way.

When Sherman and the Yankees were marching through they took all of the live stock but bothered nothing else. The buildings on the adjoining plantation were all burned. A small skirmish took place about 2 miles away from Mr. Coxton's plantation when the Yankees and Confederates met. Mr. Coxton's two sons took part in the war.

Mr. Bland was taken by Sherman's army to Savannah and then to Macon. He says that he saw President Jeff Davis give up his sword to General Sherman in surrender.

After the war Mr. Coxton was still well off in spite of the fact that he had lost quite a bit of money as a result of the war. He saved a great deal of his cash by burying it when Sherman came through. The cattle might have been saved if he (Mr. Bland could have driven them into the woods before he was seen by some of the soldiers.

At the close of the war Mr. Coxton informed all the slaves that they were free to go where they wished, but they all refused to leave. Most of them died on the plantation. Mr. Bland says that when he became of age his former master gave him a wagon, two mules a horse and buggy and ten pigs.

Mr. Bland thinks that old age is a characteristic in his family. His grandmother lived to be 115 years old and his mother 107 years old. Although in his 80's, Mr. Bland is an almost perfect picture of health. He thinks that he will live to become at least 100 years old because he is going to continue to live as sane a life as he has in the past.

RIAS BODY, EX-SLAVE.

Place of birth: Harris County, near Waverly Hall, Georgia

Date of birth: April 9, 1846

Present residence: 1419 - 24th Street, Columbus, Georgia

Interviewed: July 24, 1936

Rias Body was born the slave property of Mr. Ben Body, a Harris County planter. He states that he was about fifteen years old when the Civil War started and, many years ago, his old time white folks told him that April 9, 1846, was the date of his birth.

The "patarolers," according to "Uncle" Rias, were always quite active in ante-bellum days. The regular patrol consisted of six men who rode nightly, different planters and overseers taking turns about to do patrol duty in each militia district in the County.

All slaves were required to procure passes from their owners or their plantation overseers before they could go visiting or leave their home premises. If the "patarolers" caught a "Nigger" without a pass, they whipped him and sent him home. Sometimes, however, if the "Nigger" didn't run and told a straight story, he was let off with a lecture and a warning.

Slave children, though early taught to make themselves useful, had lots of time for playing and frolicking with the white children.

Rias was a great hand to go seining with a certain clique of white boys, who always gave him a generous or better than equal share of the fish caught.

At Christmas, every slave on the Body plantation received a present. The Negro children received candy, raisins and "nigger-toes", balls, marbles, etc.

As for food, the slaves had, with the exception of "fancy trimmins", about the same food that the whites ate. No darky in Harris County that he ever heard of ever went hungry or suffered for clothes until after freedom.

Every Saturday was a wash day. The clothes and bed linen of all Whites and Blacks went into wash every Saturday. And "Niggers", whether they liked it or not, had to "scrub" themselves every Saturday night.

The usual laundry and toilet soap was a home-made lye product, some of it a soft-solid, and some as liquid as water. The latter was stored in jugs and demijohns. Either would "fetch the dirt, or take the hide off"; in short, when applied "with rag and water, something had to come".

Many of the Body slaves had wives and husbands living on other plantations and belonging to other planters. As a courtesy to the principals of such matrimonial alliances, their owners furnished the men passes permitting them to visit their wives once or twice a week. Children born to such unions were the property of the wife's owner; the father's owner had no claim to them whatsoever.

"Uncle" Rias used to frequently come to Columbus with his master before the war, where he often saw "Niggers oxioned off" at the old slave mart which was located at what is now 1225 Broadway. Negroes to be offered for sale were driven to Columbus in droves -- like cattle -- by "Nawthon speckulatahs". And prospective buyers would visit the "block" accompanied by doctors, who would feel of, thump, and examine the "Nigger" to see if sound. A young or middle-aged Negro man, specially or even well trained in some trade or out-of-th-ordinary line of work, often sold for from $2000.00 to $4000.00 in gold. Women and "runty Nigger men" commanded a price of from $600.00 up, each. A good "breedin oman", though, says "Uncle" Rias, would sometimes sell for as high as $1200.00.

Rias Body had twelve brothers, eight of whom were "big buck Niggers," and older than himself. The planters and "patarolers" accorded these "big Niggers" unusual privileges -- to the end that he estimates that they "wuz de daddies uv least a hunnert head o' chillun in Harris County before de war broke out." Some of these children were "scattered" over a wide area.

Sin, according to Rias Body, who voices the sentiment of the great majcrity of aged Negroes, is that, or everything, which one does and says "not in the name of the Master". The holy command, "Whatever ye do, do it in My name," is subjected to some very unorthodox interpretations by many members of the colored race. Indeed, by their peculiar interpretation of this command, it is established that "two clean sheets can't smut", which means that a devout man and woman may indulge in the primal passion without committing sin.

The old man rather boasts of the fact that he received a number of whippings when a slave: says he now knows that he deserved them, "an thout 'em", he would have no doubt "been hung 'fore he wuz thutty years ole."

Among the very old slaves whom he knew as a boy were quite a few whom the Negroes looked up to, respected, and feared as witches, wizzards, and magic-workers. These either brought their "learnin" with them from Africa or absorbed it from their immediate African forebears. Mentally, these people wern't brilliant, but highly sensitized, and Rias gave "all sich" as wide a berth as opportunity permitted him, though he knows "dat dey had secret doins an carrying-ons". In truth, had the Southern Whites not curbed the mumbo-jumboism of his people, he is of the opinion that it would not now be safe to step "out his doe at night".

Incidentally, Rias Body is more fond of rabbit than any other meat "in de wurrul", and says that he could -- if he were able to get them -- eat three rabbits a day, 365 days in the year, and two for breakfast on Christmas morning. He also states that pork, though killed in the hottest of July weather, will not spoil if it is packed down in shucked corn-on-the-cob. This he learned in slavery days when, as a "run-away", he "knocked a shoat in the head" one summer and tried it -- proving it.

EX-SLAVE INTERVIEW:

JAMES BOLTON
ATHENS, GEORGIA

Written by: Mrs. Sarah H. Hall,
Federal Writers'
Project, Residency 4,
Athens, Georgia.

Edited by: Miss Maude Barragan,
Federal Writers' Project,
Residency 13,
Augusta, Georgia.

JAMES BOLTON

ATHENS, GEORGIA

"It never was the same on our plantation atter we done laid Mistess away," said James Bolton, 85 year old mulatto ex-slave. "I ain't never forget when Mistess died - she had been so good to every nigger on our plantation. When we got sick, Mistess allus had us tended to. The niggers on our plantation all walked to church to hear her funeral sermon and then walked to the graveyard to the buryin'."

James, shrivelled and wrinkled, with his bright eyes taking in everything on one of his rare visits to town, seemed glad of the chance to talk about slavery days. He spoke of his owner as "my employer" and hastily corrected himself by saying, "I means, my marster."

"My employer, I means my marster, and my mistess, they was sho' all right white folkses," he continued. "They lived in the big 'ouse. Hit was all painted brown. I heard tell they was more'n 900 acres in our plantation and lots of folkses lived on it. The biggest portion was woods. "My paw, he was name Whitfield Bolton and Liza Bolton was my maw. Charlie, Edmund, Thomas and John Bolton was my brothers and I had one sister, she was Rosa. We belonged to Marse Whitfield Bolton and we lived on his plantation in Oglethorpe County near Lexington, not far from the Wilkes County line.

"We stayed in a one room log cabin with a dirt floor. A frame made outen pine poles was fastened to the wall to hold up the mattresses. Our mattresses was made outen cotton bagging stuffed with wheat straw. Our kivers was quilts made outen old clothes. Slave 'omans too old to work in the fields made the quilts.

"Maw, she went up to the big house one't a week to git the 'lowance or vittles. They 'lowanced us a week's rations at a time. Hit were generally hog meat, corn meal and sometimes a little flour. Maw, she done our cookin' on the coals in the fire-place at our cabin. We had plenty of 'possums and rabbits and fishes and sometimes we had wild tukkeys and partidges. Slaves warn't spozen to go huntin' at night and everybody know you can't ketch no 'possums 'ceppin' at night! Jus' the same, we had plenty 'possums and nobody ax how we cotch 'em!" James laughed and nodded. "Now, 'bout them rabbits! Slaves warn't 'lowed to have no guns and no dogs of they own. All the dogs on our plantation belonged to my employer- I means, to my marster, and he 'lowed us to use his dogs to run down the rabbits. Nigger mens and boys 'ud go in crowds, sometimes as many as twelve at one time, and a rabbit ain't got no chance 'ginst a lot of niggers and dogs when they light out fer to run 'im down!

"What wild critters we wanted to eat and couldn't run down, we was right smart 'bout ketchin' in traps. We cotch lots of wild tukkeys and partidges in traps and nets. Long Crick runned through our plantation and the river warn't no fur piece off. We sho' did ketch the fishes, mostly cats, and perch and heaps and heaps of suckers. We cotch our fishes mos'n generally with hook and line, but the carpenters on our plantation knowed how to make basket traps that sho' nuff did lay in the fishes! God only knows how long it's been since this old nigger pulled a big shad out of the river. Ain't no shads been cotch in the river round here in so long I disremembers when!

"We didn' have no gardens of our own round our cabins. My employer-- I means, my marster-- had one big gyarden for our whole plantation and all his niggers had to work in it whensomever he wanted 'em to, then he give 'em all plenty good gyarden sass for theyselfs. They was collards and cabbage and turnips and beets and english peas and beans and onions, and they was allus some garlic for ailments. Garlic was mostly to cure wums (worms). They roasted the garlic in the hot ashes and squez the juice outen it and made the chilluns take it. Sometimes they made poultices outen garlic for the pneumony.

"We saved a heap of bark from wild cherry and poplar and black haw and slippery ellum trees and we dried out mullein leaves. They was all mixed and brewed to make bitters. Whensomever a nigger got sick, them bitters was good for - well ma'am, they was good for what ailed 'em! We tuk 'em for rheumatiz, for fever, and for the misery in the stummick and for most all sorts of sickness. Red oak bark tea was good for sore throat.

"I never seed no store bought clothes twel long atter freedom done come! One slave 'oman done all the weavin' in a separate room called the 'loom house.' The cloth was dyed with home-made coloring. They used indigo for blue, red oak bark for brown, green husks offen warnicks (walnuts) for black, and sumacs for red and they'd mix these colors to make other colors. Other slave 'omans larned to sew and they made all the clothes. Endurin' the summer-time we jus' wore shirts and pants made outen plain cotton cloth. They wove wool in with the cotton to make the cloth for our winter clothes. The wool was raised right thar on our plantation. We had our own shoemaker man- he was a slave named Buck Bolton and he made all the shoes the niggers on our plantation wore.

"I waren't nothin' but chillun when freedom come. In slavery-time chilluns waren't 'lowed to do no wuk kazen the marsters wanted they niggers to grow up big and strong and didn' want 'em stunted none. Tha's howcome I didn' git no mo' beatin's than I did! My employer- I means, my marster, never did give me but one lickin'. He had done told me to watch the cows and keep 'em in the pastur'. I cotch lots of grasshoppers and started fishin' in the crick runnin' through the pastur' and fust thing I knowed, the overseer was roundin' up all the other niggers to git the cows outen the cornfields! I knowed then my time had done come!"

James was enjoying the spotlight now, and his audience did not have to prompt him. Plantation recollections crowded together in his old mind.

"We had one overseer at a time," he said, "and he allus lived at the big 'ouse. The overseers warn't quality white folkses like our marster and mistess but we never heard nuffin' 'bout no poor white trash in them days, and effen we had heard sumpin' like that we'd have knowed better'n to let Marster hear us make such talk! Marster made us call his overseer 'Mister.' We had one overseer named Mr. Andrew Smith and another time we had a overseer named Mr.

Pope Short. Overseers was jus' there on the business of gettin' the work done - they seed atter everybody doin' his wuk 'cordin' to order.

"My employer- I means, my marster, never 'lowed no overseer to whup none of his niggers! Marster done all the whuppin' on our plantation hisself. He never did make no big bruises and he never drawed no blood, but he sho' could burn 'em up with that lash! Niggers on our plantation was whupped for laziness mostly. Next to that, whuppings was for stealin' eggs and chickens. They fed us good and plenty but a nigger is jus' bound to pick up chickens and eggs effen he kin, no matter how much he done eat! He jus' can't help it. Effen a nigger ain't busy he gwine to git into mischief!

"Now and then slaves 'ud run away and go in the woods and dig dens and live in 'em. Sometimes they runned away on 'count of cruel treatment, but most of the time they runned away kazen they jus' didn't want to wuk, and wanted to laze around for a spell. The marsters allus put the dogs atter 'em and git 'em back. They had black and brown dogs called 'nigger hounds' what waren't used for nothin' but to track down niggers.

"They waren't no such place as a jail whar we was. Effen a nigger done sumpin' disorderly they jus' natcherly tuk a lash to 'im. I ain't never seed no nigger in chains twel long atter freedom done come when I seed 'em on the chain gangs.

"The overseer woke us up at sunrise-- leas'n they called it sunrise! We would finish our vittles and be in the fields ready for wuk befo' we seed any sun! We laid off wuk at sunset and they didn't drive us hard. Leas'wise, they didn' on our plantation. I done heard they was moughty hard on 'em on other plantations. My marster never did 'low his niggers to wuk atter sundown. My employer, I means my marster, didn't have no bell. He had 'em blow bugles to wake up his hands and to call 'em from the fields. Sometimes the overseer blowed it. Mistess done larned the cook to count the clock, but none of the rest of our niggers could count the clock.

"I never knowed Marster to sell but one slave and he jus' had bought her from the market at New Orleans. She say it lonesome off on the plantation and axed Marster for to sell her to folkses livin' in town. Atter he done sold her, every time he got to town she beg 'im to buy her back! But he didn' pay her no more 'tention. When they had sales of slaves on the plantations they let everybody know what time the sale gwine to be. When the crowd git togedder they put the niggers on the block and sell 'em. Leas'wise, they call it 'puttin' on the block' - they jus' fotch 'em out and show 'em and sell 'em.

"They waren't no church for niggers on our plantation and we went to white folkses church and listened to the white preachers. We set behind a partition. Sometimes on a plantation a nigger claim he done been called to preach and effen he kin git his marster's cawn-sent he kin preach round under trees and in cabins when t'aint wuk time. These nigger preachers in slavery time was called 'chairbackers.' They waren't no chairbackers 'lowed to baptize none of Marster's niggers. White preachers done our baptizin' in Long Crick.

When we went to be baptized they allus sang, 'Amazing Grace! How sweet the sound!'"

The old negro's quavery voice rose in the familiar song. For a moment he sat thinking of those long-ago Sundays. His eyes brightened again, and he went on:

"We never done no wuk on Sundays on our plantation. The church was 'bout nine miles from the plantation and we all walked there. Anybody too old and feeble to walk the nine miles jus' stayed home, kazen Marster didn't 'low his mules used none on Sunday. All along the way niggers from other plantations 'ud jine us and sometimes befo' we git to the church house they'd be forty or fifty slaves comin' along the road in a crowd! Preaching generally lasted twel bout three o'clock. In summertime we had dinner on the ground at the church. Howsomever we didn' have no barbecue like they does now. Everybody cooked enough on Sadday and fotched it in baskets.

"I was thirty years old when I jined the church. Nobody ought to jine no church twels't he is truly borned of God, and effen he is truly borned of God he gwine know it. Effen you want a restin' place atter you leaves this old world you ought to git ready for it now!

"When folkses on our plantation died Marster allus let many of us as wanted to go, lay offen wuk twel atter the buryin'. Sometimes it were two or three months atter the buryin' befo' the funeral sermon was preached. Right now I can't rekelleck no song we sung at funerals cep'n 'Hark from the tombs a doleful sound.'

The reedy old voice carried the funeral hymn for a few minutes and then trailed off. James was thinking back into the past again.

"Spring plowin' and hoein' times we wukked all day Saddays, but mos'en generally we laid off wuk at twelve o'clock Sadday. That was dinnertime. Sadday nights we played and danced. Sometimes in the cabins, sometimes in the yards. Effen we didn' have a big stack of fat kindling wood lit up to dance by, sometimes the mens and 'omans would carry torches of kindling wood whils't they danced and it sho' was a sight to see! We danced the 'Turkey Trot' and 'Buzzard Lope', and how we did love to dance the 'Mary Jane!' We would git in a ring and when the music started we would begin wukkin' our footses while we sang 'You steal my true love and I steal your'n!'

"Atter supper we used to gether round and knock tin buckets and pans, we beat 'em like drums. Some used they fingers and some used sticks for to make the drum sounds and somebody allus blowed on quills. Quills was a row of whistles made outen reeds, or sometimes they made 'em outen bark. Every whistle in the row was a different tone and you could play any kind of tune you wants effen you had a good row of quills. They sho' did sound sweet!

"'Bout the most fun we had was at corn shuckin's whar they put the corn in long piles and called in the folkses from the plantations nigh round to shuck it. Sometimes four or five hunnert head of niggers 'ud be shuckin' corn at one time. When the corn all done been shucked they'd drink the likker the marsters give 'em and then frolic and dance from sundown to sunup. We started shuckin' corn 'bout dinnertime and tried to finish by sundown so we could have the whole night for frolic. Some years we 'ud go to ten or twelve corn shuckin's in one year!

"We would sing and pray Easter Sunday and on Easter Monday we frolicked and danced all day long! Christmas we allus had plenty good sumpin' to eat and we all got togedder and had lots of fun. We runned up to the big 'ouse early Christmas mornin' and holler out: 'Mornin', Christmas Gif'!' Then they'd give us plenty of Sandy Claus and we would go back to our cabins to have fun twel New Year's day. We knowed Christmas was over and gone when New Year's day come, kazen we got back to wuk that day atter frolickin' all Christmas week.

"We didn' know nuttin' 'bout games to play. We played with the white folkses chilluns and watched atter 'em but most of the time we played in the crick what runned through the pastur'. Nigger chilluns was allus skeered to go in the woods atter dark. Folkses done told us Raw-Head-and-Bloody Bones lived in the woods and git little chilluns and eat 'em up effen they got out in the woods atter dark!

"'Rockabye baby in the tree trops' was the onliest song I heard my maw sing to git her babies to sleep. Slave folkses sung most all the time but we didn' think of what we sang much. We jus' got happy and started singin'. Sometimes we 'ud sing effen we felt sad and lowdown, but soon as we could, we 'ud go off whar we could go to sleep and forgit all 'bout trouble!" James nodded his gray head with a wise look in his bright eyes. "When you hear a nigger singin' sad songs hit's jus' kazen he can't stop what he is doin' long enough to go to sleep!"

The laughter that greeted this sally brought an answering grin to the wrinkled old face. Asked about marriage customs, James said:

"Folkses didn' make no big to-do over weddings like they do now. When slaves got married they jus' laid down the broom on the floor and the couple jined hands and jumped back-uds over the broomstick. I done seed 'em married that way many a time. Sometimes my marster would fetch Mistess down to the slave quarters to see a weddin'. Effen the slaves gittin' married was house servants, sometimes they married on the back porch or in the back yard at the big 'ouse but plantation niggers what was field hands married in they own cabins. The bride and groom jus' wore plain clothes kazen they didn' have no more.

"When the young marsters and mistesses at the big houses got married they 'lowed the slaves to gadder on the porch and peep through the windows at the weddin'. Mos'en generally they 'ud give the young couple a slave or two to take with them to they new home. My marster's chilluns was too young to git married befo' the war was over. They was seven of them chilluns; four of 'em was gals.

"What sort of tales did they tell 'mongs't the slaves 'bout the Norf befo' the war? To tell the troof, they didn't talk much like they does now 'bout them sort of things. None of our niggers ever runned away and we didn' know nuthin' 'bout no Norf twel long atter freedom come. We visited round each other's cabins at night.

I did hear tell 'bout the patterollers. Folkses said effen they cotched niggers out at night they 'ud give 'em 'what Paddy give the drum'.

"Jus' befo' freedom comed 'bout 50 Yankee sojers come through our plantation and told us that the bull-whups and cow-hides was all dead and buried. Them sojers jus' passed on in a hurry and didn' stop for a meal or vittles or nuffin'. We didn't talk much 'bout Mr. Abbieham Lincum endurin' slavery time kazen we was skeered of him atter the war got started. I don't know nothin' 'bout Mr. Jef'son Davis, I don't remember ever hearin' 'bout him. I is heard about Mr. Booker Washin'ton and they do say he runned a moughty good school for niggers.

"One mornin' Marster blowed the bugle his own self and called us all up to the big 'ouse yard. He told us: 'You all jus' as free as I is. You are free from under the taskmarster but you ain't free from labor. You gotter labor and wuk hard effen you aims to live and eat and have clothes to wear. You kin stay here and wuk for me, or you kin go wharsomever you pleese.' He said he 'ud pay us what was right, and Lady, hit's the troof, they didn't nary a nigger on our plantation leave our marster then! I wukked on with Marster for 40 years atter the war!"

James had no fear of the Ku Klux.

"Right soon atter the war we saw plenty of Ku Kluxers but they never bothered nobody on our plantation. They allus seemed to be havin' heaps of fun. 'Course, they did have to straighten out some of them brash young nigger bucks on some of the other farms round about. Mos' of the niggers the Ku Kluxers got atter was'n on no farm, but was jus' roamin' 'round talkin' too much and makin' trouble. They had to take 'em in hand two or three times befo' some of them fool free niggers could be larned to behave theyselfs! But them Ku Kluxers kept on atter 'em twels't they larned they jus got to be good effen they 'spects to stay round here.

"Hit was about 40 years atter the war befo' many niggers 'gun to own they own lan'. They didn' know nothin' 'bout tendin' to money business when the war done ended and it take 'em a long time to lern how to buy and sell and take care of what they makes." James shook his head sadly. "Ma'am, heaps of niggers ain't never larned nothin' 'bout them things yit!

"A long time atter the war I married Lizy Yerby. I didn' give Liza no chanc't for to dress up. Jus' went and tuk her right outer the white folkses' kitchen and married her at the church in her workin' clothes. We had 13 chilluns but they ain't but two of 'em livin' now. Mos' of our chilluns died babies. Endurin' slavery Mistess tuk care of all the nigger babies borned on our plantations and looked atter they mammies too, but atter freedom come heap of nigger babies died out.

James said he had two wives, both widows.

"I married my second wife 37 years ago. To tell the troof, I don't rightly know how many grandchilluns I got, kazen I ain't seed some of 'em for thirty years. My chilluns is off fum here and I wouldn' know to save my life whar they is or what they does. My sister and brothers they is done dead out what ain't gone off, I don't know for sho' whar none of 'em is now.

A sigh punctuated James' monologue, and his old face was shadowed by a look of fear.

"Now I gwine tell you the troof. Now that it's all over I don't find life so good in my old age, as it was in slavery time when I was chillun down on Marster's plantation. Then I didn' have to worry 'bout whar my clothes and my somepin' to eat was comin' from or whar I was gwine to sleep. Marster tuk keer of all that. Now I ain't able for to wuk and make a livin' and hit's sho' moughty hard on this old nigger."

ALEC BOSTWICK
Ex-Slave - Age 76.

All of Uncle Alec Bostwick's people are dead and he lives in his tiny home with a young Negress named Emma Vergal. It was a beautiful April morning when his visitor arrived and while he was cordial enough he seemed very reluctant about talking. However, as one question followed another his interest gradually overcame his hesitancy and he began to unfold his life's story.

"I wuz born in Morgan County, an' I warn't mo' dan four year old when de War ended so I don't ricollect nothin' 'bout slav'ry days. I don't know much 'bout my ma, but her name was Martha an' pa's name was Jordan Bostwick, I don't know whar dey come from. When I knowed nothin' I wuz dar on de plantation. I had three brothers; George, John an' Reese, an' dey's all dead. I dis'members my sister's name. Dar warn't but one gal an' she died when she wuz little.

"Ain't much to tell 'bout what wuz done in de quarters. Slaves wuz gyarded all de time jus' lak Niggers on de chain gang now. De overseer always sot by wid a gun.

"'Bout de beds, Nigger boys didn't pay no 'tention to sich as dat 'cause all dey keered 'bout wuz a place to sleep but 'peers lak to me dey wuz corded beds, made wid four high posties, put together wid iron pegs, an' holes what you run de cords thoo', bored in de sides. De cords wuz made out of b'ar grass woun' tight together. Dey put straw an' old quilts on 'em, an' called 'em beds.

"Gran'pa Berry wuz too old to wuk in de field so he stayed 'roun' de house an' piddled. He cut up wood, tended to de gyarden an' yard, an' bottomed chairs. Gran'ma Liza done de cookin' an' nussed de white folkses chilluns.

"I wukked in de field 'long side de rest of de Niggers, totin' water an' sich lak, wid de overseer dar all de time wid dat gun.

"What you talkin' 'bout Miss? Us didn't have no money. Sho' us didn't. Dey had to feed us an' plenty of it, 'cause us couldn't wuk if dey didn't feed us good.

"Us et cornbread, sweet 'tatoes, peas, home-made syrup an' sich lak. De meat wuz fried sometimes, but mos' of de time it wuz biled wid de greens. All de somethin' t'eat wuz cooked in de fireplace. Dey didn't know what stoves wuz in dem days. Yes Ma'am, us went 'possum huntin' at night, an' us had plenty 'possums too. Dey put sweet 'tatoes an' fat meat 'roun' 'em, an' baked 'em in a oven what had eyes on each side of it to put hooks in to take it off de fire wid.

"No Ma'am, us didn't go fishin', or rabbit huntin' nuther. Us had to wuk an' warn't no Nigger 'lowed to do no frolickin' lak dat in daytime. De white folkses done all de fishin' an' day-time huntin'. I don't 'member lakin' no sartin' somethin'. I wuz jus' too glad to git anythin'. Slaves didn't have no gyardens of dey own. Old Marster had one big gyarden what all de slaves et out of.

"Tell you 'bout our clo'es: us wore home-made clo'es, pants an' shirts made out of cotton in summer an' in de winter dey give us mo' home-made clo'es only dey wuz made of wool. All de clawf wuz made on de loom right dar on de plantation. Us wore de same things on Sunday what us did in de week, no diffunt. Our shoes wuz jus' common brogans what dey made at home. I ain't seed no socks 'til long atter de War. Co'se some folkses mought a had 'em, but us didn't have none.

"Marster Berry Bostwick an' Mist'ess Mary Bostwick, had a passel of chillun, I don't 'member none 'cept young Marse John. De others drifted off an' didn't come back, but young Marse John stayed on wid Old Marster an' Old Mist'ess 'til dey died. Old Marster, he warn't good. Truth is de light, an' he wuz one mean white man. Old Mist'ess wuz heaps better dan him. Dar wuz 'bout 150 mens an' 75 'omans. I couldn't keep up wid de chilluns. Dere wuz too many for me.

"Marster an' Mist'ess lived in a big fine house, but de slave quarters wuz made of logs, 'bout de size of box cyars wid two rooms.

"'Bout dat overseer he wuz a mean man, if one ever lived. He got de slaves up wid a gun at five o'clock an' wukked 'em 'til way atter sundown, standin' right over 'em wid a gun all de time. If a Nigger lagged or tuk his eyes off his wuk, right den an' dar he would make him strip down his clo'es to his waist, an' he whup him wid a cat-o-nine tails. Evvy lick dey struck him meant he wuz hit nine times, an' it fotch de red evvy time it struck.

"Oh! Yes Ma'am, dey had a cyar'iage driver, he didn't do much 'cept look atter de hawses an' drive de white folkses 'roun'.

"I done tole you 'bout dat overseer; all he done wuz sot 'roun' all day wid a gun an' make de Niggers wuk. But I'se gwine tell you de trufe, he sho' wuz poor white trash wid a house full of snotty-nose chilluns. Old Marster tole him he wuz jus' lak a rabbit, he had so many chillun. I means dis; if dem days comes back I hope de good Lord takes me fus'.

"Dey had a house whar dey put de Niggers, what wuz called de gyard house, an' us didn't know nothin' 'bout no jail dat day an' time. I seed 'em drive de Niggers by old Marster's place in droves takin' 'em to Watkinsville. Morgan County, whar us lived, touched Oconee an' dat wuz the nighes' town. One day I went wid old Marster to Watkinsville an' I seed 'em sell Niggers on de block. I warn't sold. When I knowed nothin' I wuz right whar I wuz at.

"No Ma'am, dey warn't no schools for de Niggers in dem days. If a Nigger wuz seed wid a paper, de white folks would pretty nigh knock his head off him.

"Us didn't have no church in de country for Niggers, an' dey went to church wid deir white folkses, if dey went a tall. De white folks sot in front, an' de Niggers sot in de back. All de time dat overseer wuz right dar wid his gun. When dey baptized de Niggers dey tuk 'em down to de river and plunged 'em in, while dem what had done been baptized sang: "Dar's a Love Feast in Heb'en Today."

"Yes Ma'am, de white folkses had deir cemetery, an' dey had one for de slaves. When dere wuz a funeral 'mong de Niggers us sung:

'Dark was de night
And cold was de groun'
Whar my Marster was laid
De drops of sweat
Lak blood run down
In agony He prayed.'

"Dem coffins sho' wuz mournful lookin' things, made out of pine boa'ds an' painted wid lampblack; dey wuz black as de night. Dey wuz big at de head an' little at de foot, sort a lak airplanes is. De inside wuz lined wid white clawf, what dey spun on de plantation.

"De patterollers wuz right on dey job. Slaves use' to frame up on 'em if dey knowed whar dey wuz hidin', 'waitin' to cotch a Nigger. Dey would git hot ashes an' dash over 'em, an' dem patterollers dey sho' would run, but de slaves would git worse dan dat, if dey was cotched.

"Miss, in slav'ry time when Niggers come from de fields at night dey warn't no frolickin'. Dey jus' went to sleep. De mens wukked all day Sadday, but de 'omans knocked off at twelve o'clock to wash an' sich lak.

"Christmas times dey give us a week off an' brung us a little candy an' stuff 'roun'. Not much, not much. On New Year's Day us had to git back on de job.

"Chilluns what wuz big enough to wuk didn't have time in week days to play no games on Marse Bostwick's place. On Sunday us played wid marbles made out of clay, but dat's all. I heered my Ma sing a little song to de baby what soun' lak dis:

'Hush little baby
Don't you cry
You'll be an angel
Bye-an'-bye.'

"Yes Ma'am, dere wuz one thing dey wuz good 'bout. When de Niggers got sick dey sont for de doctor. I heered 'em say dey biled jimson weeds an' made tea for colds, an' rhubarb tea wuz to cure worms in chillun. I wuz too young to be bothered 'bout witches an' charms, Rawhead an' Bloody Bones an' sich. I didn't take it in.

"When de Yankees come thoo' an' 'lowed us wuz free, us thought dey wuz jus' dem patterollers, an' us made for de woods. Dey tole us to come out, dat us wuz free Niggers. Marster Berry said: 'You dam Niggers am free. You don't b'long to me no more.

"Us married long time atter de War, an' us had a little feast: cake, wine, fried chicken, an' ham, an' danced 'til 'mos' daybreak. I 'members how good she looked wid dat pretty dove colored dress, all trimmed wid lace. Us didn't have no chillun. She wuz lak a tree what's sposen to bear fruit an' don't. She died 'bout thirteen years ago.

"When de Ku Kluxers come thoo', us chillun thought de devil wuz atter us for sho'. I wuz sich a young chap I didn't take in what dey said 'bout Mr. Abyham Lincoln, an' Mr. Jeff Davis. Us would a been slaves 'til yit, if Mr. Lincoln hadn't sot us free. Dey wuz bofe of 'em, good mens. I sho' had ruther be free. Who wants a gun over 'em lak a prisoner? A pusson is better off dead.

"I jined de church 'cause dis is a bad place at de bes'

an' dere's so many mean folkses, what's out to seem good an' ain't. An' if you serve God in de right way, I'se sho' when you die he'll give you a place to rest for evermore. An' 'cordin' to my notion dat's de way evvybody oughta live.

In conclusion, Alec said: "I don't want to talk no more. I'se disappointed, I thought sho' you wuz one of dem pension ladies what come for to fetch me some money. I sho' wish dey would come. Good-bye Miss." Then he hobbled into the house.

Barragan - Harris

NANCY BOUDRY, THOMSON, GEORGIA

"If I ain't a hunnerd," said Nancy, nodding her white-turbaned head, "I sho' is close to it, 'cause I got a grandson 50 years old."

Nancy's silky white hair showed long and wavy under her headband. Her gingham dress was clean, and her wrinkled skin was a reddish-yellow color, showing a large proportion of Indian and white blood. Her eyes were a faded blue.

"I speck I is mos' white," acknowledged Nancy, "but I ain't never knowed who my father was. My mother was a dark color."

The cottage faced the pine grove behind an old church. Pink ramblers grew everywhere, and the sandy yard was neatly kept. Nancy's paralyzed granddaughter-in-law hovered in the doorway, her long smooth braids hanging over Indian-brown shoulders, a loose wrapper of dark blue denim flowing around her tall unsteady figure. She was eager to take part in the conversation but hampered by a thick tongue induced, as Nancy put it, "by a bad sore throat she ain't got over."

Nancy's recollections of plantation days were colored to a somber hue by overwork, childbearing, poor food and long working hours.

"Master was a hard taskmaster," said Nancy. "My husband didn' live on de same plantation where I was, de Jerrell place in Columbia County. He never did have nuthin' to give me 'cause he never got nuthin'. He had to come and ask my white folks for me. Dey had to carry passes everywhar dey went, if dey didn't, dey'd git in trouble.

"I had to work hard, plow and go and split wood jus' like a man. Sometimes dey whup me. Dey whup me bad, pull de cloes off down to de wais' - my master did it, our folks didn' have overseer.

"We had to ask 'em to let us go to church. Went to white folks church, "'tell de black folks get one of dere own. No'm, I dunno how to read. Never had no schools at all, didn' 'low us to pick up a piece of paper and look at it."

"Nancy, wasn't your mistress kind to you?"

"Mistis was sorta kin' to me, sometimes. But dey only give me meat and bread, didn' give me nothin' good - I ain' gwine tell no story. I had a heap to undergo wid. I had to scour at night at de Big House - two planks one night, two more de nex'. De women peoples spun at night and reeled, so many cuts a night. Us had to git up befo' daybreak be ready to go to de fiel's.

"My master didn' have but three cullud people, dis yuh man what I stayed wid, my young master, had not been long married and dus' de han's dey give him when he marry was all he had.

"Didn' have no such house as dis," Nancy looked into the open door of the comfortable cottage, "sometimes dey have a house built, it would be daubed. Dus' one family, didn' no two families double up."

"But the children had a good time, didn't they? They played games?"

"Maybe dey did play ring games, I never had no time to see what games my chillun play, I work so hard. Heap o' little chillun slep' on de flo'. Never had no frolics neither, no ma'm, and didn' go to none. We would have prayer meetings on Saturday nights, and one night in de week us had a chairback preacher, and sometimes a regular preacher would come in."

Nancy did not remember ever having seen the Patterollers.

"I hearn talk of 'em you know, heap o' times dey come out and make out like dey gwine shoot you at night, dey mus' been Patterollers, dey was gettin' hold of a heap of 'em."

"What did you do about funerals, Nancy?"

"Dey let us knock off for funerals, I tell de truth. Us stay up all night, singin' and prayin'. Dey make de coffin outter pine boards."

"Did you suffer during the war?"

"We done de bes' we could, we et what we could get, sometimes didn' have nothin' to eat but piece of cornbread, but de white folks allus had chicken."

"But you had clothes to wear?"

"Us had clothes 'cause we spun de thread and weaved 'em. Dey bought dem dere great big ole brogans where you couldn' hardly walk in 'em. Not like dese shoes I got on." Nancy thrust out her foot, easy in "Old Ladies' Comforts."

"When they told you were free, Nancy, did the master appear to be angry?"

"No'm, white folks didn' 'pear to be mad. My master dus' tole us we was free. Us moved right off, but not so far I couldn' go backwards and forwards to see 'um." (So it was evident that even if Nancy's life had been hard, there was a bond between her and her former owners.) "I didn' do no mo' work for 'um, I work for somebody else. Us rented land and made what we could, so we could have little somethin' to eat. I scoured and waited on white people in town, got little piece of money, and was dus' as proud!"

Nancy savored the recollection of her first earned money a moment, thinking back to the old days.

"I had a preacher for my second marriage," she continued. "Fo' chillum died on me - one girl, de yuthers was babies. White doctor tended me."

Asked about midwifery, Nancy smiled.

"I was a midwife myself, to black and white, after freedom. De Thomson doctors all liked me and tole people to 'git Nancy.' I used 'tansy tea' - heap o' little root - made black pepper tea, fotch de pains on 'em. When I would git to de place where I had a hard case, I would send for de doctor, and he would help me out, yes, doctor holp me out of all of 'em."

Asked about signs and superstitions, Nancy nodded.

"I have seed things. Dey look dus' like a person, walkin' in de woods. I would look off and look back to see it again and it be gone." Nancy lowered her voice mysteriously, and looked back into the little room where Vanna's unsteady figure moved from bed to chair. "I seed a coffin floatin' in de air in dat room - - " she shivered, "and I heard a heap o' knockings. I dunno what it bees - but de sounds come in de house. I runs ev'y squeech owl away what comes close, too." Nancy clasped her hands, right thumb over left thumb, "does dat - and it goes on away - dey quits hollerin', you chokin' 'em when you does dat."

"Do you plant by the moon, Nancy?"

"Plant when de moon change, my garden, corn, beans. I planted some beans once on de wrong time of de moon and ey didn' bear nothing – I hated it so bad, I didn' know what to do, so I been mindful ever since when I plant. Women peoples come down on de moon, too. I ain't know no signs to raise chillun. I whup mine when dey didn' do right, I sho' did. I didn' 'low my chillun to take nothin' – no aigs and nothin' 'tall and bring 'em to my house. I say 'put dem right whar you git 'em."

"Did you sing spirituals, Nancy?"

"I sang regular meetin' songs," she said, "like 'lay dis body down' and 'let yo' joys be known' – but I can't sing now, not any mo'."

Nancy was proud of her quilt-making ability.

"Git 'um, Vanna, let de ladies see 'um," she said; and when Vanna brought the gay pieces made up in a "double-burst" (sunburst) pattern, Nancy fingered the squares with loving fingers. "Hit's pooty, ain't it?" she asked wistfully, "I made one for a white lady two years ago, but dey hurts my fingers now – makes 'em stiff."

100141

FOLKLORE INTERVIEW

ALICE BRADLEY
Hull Street near Corner of Hoyt Street,
Athens, Georgia

KIZZIE COLQUITT
243 Macon Avenue,
Athens, Georgia.

Written by: Miss Grace McCune
Athens, Georgia.

Edited by: Mrs. Leila Harris
Editor,
Federal Writers' Project,
Augusta, Georgia.

ALICE BRADLEY, or "Aunt Alice" as she is known to everybody, "runs cards" and claims to be a seeress. Apologetic and embarrassed because she had overslept and was straightening her room, she explained that she hadn't slept well because a dog had howled all night and she was uneasy because of this certain forerunner of disaster.

"Here t'is Sunday mornin' and what wid my back, de dog, and de rheumatics in my feets, its ~~done~~ too late to go to church, so come in honey I'se glad to hab somebody to talk to. Dere is sho' goin' to be a corpse close 'round here. One night a long time ago two dogs howled all night long and on de nex' Sunday dere wuz two corpses in de church at de same time. Dat's one sign dat neber fails, when a dog howls dat certain way somebody is sho' goin' to be daid."

When asked what her full name was, she said: "My whole name is Alice Bradley now. I used to be a Hill, but when I married dat th'owed me out of bein' a Hill, so I'se jus' a Bradley now. I wuz born on January 14th but I don't 'member what year. My ma had three chillun durin' de war and one jus' atter de war. I think dat las' one wuz me, but I ain't sho'. My pa's name wuz Jim Hill, and my ma's name wuz Ca'line Hill. Both of 'em is daid now. Pa died October 12, 1896 and wuz 88 years old. Ma died November 20, 1900; she wuz 80 years old. I knows dem years is right 'cause I got 'em from dat old fambly Bible so I kin git 'em jus' right. One of my sisters, older dan I is, stays in Atlanta wid her son. Since she los' one of her sons, her mind's done gone. My other sister ain't as old as I is but her mind is all right and she is well.

"I wuz raised in Washin'ton, Wilkes County, and de fust I 'members wuz stayin' wid Miss Alice Rayle. She had three chillun and I nussed 'em. One of de boys is a doctor now, and has a fambly of his own, and de las' I heered of 'im, he wuz stayin' in Atlanta.

"I'se been married two times. I runned away wid Will Grisham, when I wuz 'bout 14 years old. Mr. Carter, a Justice of de Peace, met us under a 'simmon tree and tied de knot right dar. My folks ketched us, but us wuz already married and so it didn't make no diffunce.

"I lived on a farm wid my fust husband, and us had three chillun, but dey is all gone now. I 'members when my oldes' gal wuz 'bout 2 years old, dey wuz playin' out on de porch wid dey little dog, when a mad dog come by and bit my chillun's dog. Folks kilt our dog, and jus' 'bout one week atterwards my little gal wuz daid too. She did love dat little dog, and he sho' did mind 'er. She jus' grieved herself to death 'bout dat dog.

"Atter my fust husband died, I married Rich Bradley. Rich wuz a railroad man, and he went off to Washin'ton, D. C., to wuk. He sont me money all de time den, but when he went from dar to Shecargo to wuk I didn't hear from 'im long, and I don't know what's happened to 'im 'til now, for it's been a long time since I heered from 'im.

"I loves to run de cyards for my friends. I always tells 'em when I sees dere's trouble in de cyards for 'em, and shows 'em how to git 'round it, if I kin. None of de res' of my folks ever run de cyards, but I'se been at it ever since I wuz jus' a little gal, pickin' up old wore out cyards, dat had been th'owed away, 'cause I

Could see things in 'em. I 'members one time when I wuz small and didn't know so good what de cyards wuz tellin' me, dat a rich man, one of de riches' in Wilkes County, wuz at our place, I tol 'im de cyards when I run 'em. I saw sompin' wuz goin' to happen on his place, dat two colored mens would be tangled up wid, but I didn't know jus' what wuz goin' to happen. And sho' 'nuff, two colored mens sot fire to his bards and burned up all his horses and mules, de onlies' thing dey saved wuz one ridin' horse. Dey ketched de mens, and dey served time for what dey done. One of 'em died way out yonder where dey sont 'em.

"I 'members one white lady way out in Alabama sont a note axin' me to run de cyards for her. I runned 'em and got one of my friends to writer her what I seed. Day had run bright and dat wuz good luck. One time I runned de cyards for two sisters dat had done married two brothers, and de cyards run so close kin date I wuz able to tell 'em how dey wuz married and dey tol me dat I wuz right.

"And jus' a few days ago a old man come to see me thinkin' dat he wuz pizened. When I runned de cyards, I seed his trouble. He had been drinkin' and wuz sick, so I jus' give him a big dose of soda and cream of tartar and he got better. Den I tole him to go on home; dat nobody hadn't done nothin' to 'im and all he needed wuz a little medicine.

"I told Mr. Dick Armell of how he wuz goin' to git kilt if he went up in his airyplane dat day and begged him not to try it but to wait. He wouldn't listen and went on and got kilt jus' lak I tole 'im he would. I runned de cyards for Mrs. Armell lots of times for I liked 'im, and he wuz a fine man. I runned de cyards for 'im one time 'fore he went to de World's Fair, and de cyards run bright, and his trip wuz a good one jus' lak I tole 'im it would be.

"All de old white folks dat I wuz raised up wid, de Hills from Washin'ton, Wilkes, is gone now, 'cept I think one of de gals is wukin' at de capitol in Atlanta, but she done married now and I don't 'member her name."

Alice excused herself to answer a knock at the door. Upon her return she said: "Dat wuz one of my white chillun. I wukked for 'em so long and one of 'em comes by every now an' den to see if I needs sompin'. Her ma done had a new picture of herself took and wanted me to see it. Dey sho' is good to me."

Alice doesn't charge for "running the cards." She says she doesn't have a license, and is very thankful for anything that visitors may care to give her. She will not run the cards on Sunday. "Dat's bad luck," she said. "Come back some day when tain't Sunday, and I'll see whats in de cyards for you!"

Old Aunt KIZZIE COLQUITT, about 75 years old, was busily washing in her neat kitchen. She opened the door and window frequently to let out the smoke, saying: "Dis old wore out stove don't draw so good." Her hands and feet were badly swollen and she seemed to be suffering.

"I'll be glad to tell all I kin 'member 'bout dem old times," she said. "I wuz borned durin' de war, but I don't 'member what year. My pa wuz Mitchell Long. He b'longed to Marster Sam Long of Elbert

County. Us lived on Broad River. My ma wuz Sallie Long, and she b'longed to Marster Billie Lattimore. Dey stayed on de other side of Broad River and my pa and ma had to cross de river to see one another. Atter de war wuz over, and dey wuz free, my pa went to Jefferson, Georgia, and dar he died.

"My ma married some nigger from way out in Indiana. He promised her he would send money back for her chillun, but us never heered nothin' from 'im no mo'. I wuz wid' my w'ite folks, de Lattimores, when my ma died, way out in Indiana.

"Atter Marse Bob died, I stayed wid my old Missus, and slep' by her bed at night. She wuz good to me, and de hardes' wuk I done wuz pickin' up acorns to fatten de hogs. I stayed dar wid her 'til she died. Us had plenty t'eat, a smokehouse filled wid hams, and all de other things us needed. Dey had a great big fireplace and a big old time oven whar dey baked bread, and it sho' wuz good bread.

"My old Missus died when I wuz 'bout 6 years old, and I wuz sont to Lexin'ton, Georgia, to live wid my sister. Dere wuz jus' de two of us chilluns. Den us wukked every day, and went to bed by dark; not lak de young folks now, gallivantin' 'bout all night long.

"When I wuz 'bout 14 I married and come to live on Dr. Willingham's place. It wuz a big plantation, and dey really lived. When de crops wuz all in and all de wuk done, dey had big times 'round dar.

"Dere wuz de corn shuckin' wid one house for de corn and another house for de shucks. Atter all de shuckin' wuz done, dere wuz eatin' and dancin'. And it wuz eatin' too! Dey kilt hogs, barbecued 'em, and roasted some wid apples in dey mouf's to give 'em a good flavor, and course a little corn likker went wid it. Dey had big doin's at syrup makin' time too, but dat wuz hard wuk den. Makin' syrup sho' wuz a heap of trouble.

"Later us lived wid de Johnson fambly, and atter my old man died, I come to dis town wid de Johnsons. Dere wuz three chilluns, Percy, Lewis, and a gal. I stayed wid 'em 'til de chilluns wuz all growed up and eddicated. All my other w'ite folks is gone; my sister done gone too, and my son; all de chillun dat I had, deys done daid too.

"Now I has to wash so I kin live. I used to have plenty, but times is changed and now sometimes I don't have nothin' but bread, and jus' bread is hard to git, heap of de time.

"I put in for one of dem old age pensions, but dey ain't give me nothin' yet, so I jus' wuk when I kin, and hope dat it won't be long 'fore I has plenty again."

JUL 28 1937

OLD SLAVE STORY

DELLA BRISCOE

MACON, GEORGIA.

By Adella S. Dixon (Colored)

Della Briscoe, now living in Macon, is a former slave of Mr. David Ross, who owned a large plantation in Putnam County. Della, when a very tiny child, was carried there with her father and mother, Sam and Mary Ross. Soon after their arrival the mother was sent to work at the "big house" in Eatonton. This arrangement left Della, her brother and sister to the care of their grandmother, who really posed as their mother. The children grew up under the impression that their mother was an older sister and did not know the truth until just after the close of the Civil War, when the mother became seriously ill and called the children to her bedside to tell them goodbye.

Mr. David Ross had a large family and was considered the richest planter in the county. Nearly every type of soil was found on his vast estate, composed of hilly sections as well as acres of lowlands. The highway entering Eatonton divided the plantation and, down this road every Friday, Della's father drove the wagon to town with a supply of fresh butter, for Mrs. Ross' thirty head of cows supplied enough milk to furnish the city dwellers with butter.

Refrigeration was practically unknown, so a well was used to keep the butter fresh. This cool well was eighty feet deep and passed through a layer of solid rock. A rope ladder was suspended from the mouth of the well to the place where the butter was lowered for preservation. For safety, and to shield it from the sun, reeds were planted all around the well. And as they grew very tall, a stranger would not suspect a well being there.

In addition to marketing, Della's father trapped beavers which were plentiful in the swampy part of the plantation bordering the Oconee, selling their pelts to traders in the nearby towns of Augusta and Savannah, where Mr. Ross also marketed his cotton and large quantities of corn. Oxen, instead of mules, were used to make the trips to market and return, each trip consuming six or seven days.

The young children were assigned small tasks, such as piling brush in "new grounds", carrying water to field hands, and driving the calves to pasture.

Punishment was administered, though not as often as on some plantations. The little girl, Della, was whipped only once -- for breaking up a turkey's nest she had found. Several were accused of this, and because the master could not find the guilty party, he whipped each of the children.

Crime was practically unknown and Mr. Ross' slaves never heard of a jail until they were freed.

Men were sometimes placed in "bucks", which meant they were laid across blocks with their hand and feet securely tied. An iron bar was run between the blocks to prevent any movement; then, after being stripped, they were whipped. Della said that she knew of but one case of this type of punishment being administered a Ross slave.

Sickness was negligible -- childbirth being practically the only form of a Negro woman's "coming down".

As a precaution against disease, a tonic was given each slave every spring. Three were also, every spring, taken from the field each day until every one had been given a dose of calomel and salts. Mr. Ross once bought two slaves who became ill with smallpox soon after their arrival. They were isolated in a small house located in the center of a field, while one other slave was sent there to nurse them. All three were burned to death when their hut was destroyed by fire.

In case of death, even on a neighboring place, all work was suspended until the dead was buried.

Sunday, the only day of rest, was often spent in attending religious services, and because these were irregularly held, brush arbor meetings were common. This arbor was constrcuted of a brush roof supported by posts and crude joists. The seats were usually made of small saplings nailed to short stumps.

Religion was greatly stressed and every child was christened shortly after its birth. An adult who desired to join the church went first to the master to obtain his permission. He was then sent to the home of a minister who lived a short distance away at a place called Flat Rock. Here, his confession was made and, at the next regular service, he was formally received into the church.

Courtships were brief.

The "old man", who was past the age for work and only had to watch what went on at the quarters, was usually the first to notice a budding friendship, which he reported to the master. The couple was then questioned and, if they consented, were married without the benefit of clergy.

Food was distributed on Monday night, and for each adult slave the following staple products were allowed - - -

Weekly ration:	On Sunday:
3½ lbs. meat	One qt. syrup
1 pk. of meal	One gal. flour
1 gal. shorts	One cup lard

Vegetables, milk, etc., could be obtained at the "big house", but fresh meat and chickens were never given. The desire for these delicacies often overcame the slaves' better natures, and some frequently went night foraging for small shoats and chickens.

The "old man" kept account of the increase or decrease in live stock and poultry and reported anything missing each day. When suspicion fell on a visitor of the previous night, this information was given to his master, who then searched the accused's dinner pail and cabin. If meat was found in either the culprit was turned over to his accuser for punishment. After being whipped, he was forbidden for three months to visit the plantation where he had committed the theft.

One of Della's grandmother's favorite recipes was made of dried beef and wheat. The wheat was brought from the field and husked by hand. This, added to the rapidly boiling beef, was cooked until a mush resulted, which was then eaten from wooden bowls with spoons of the same material. White plates were never used by the slaves.

Cloth for clothing was woven on the place. Della's grandmother did most of the spinning, and she taught her child to spin when she was so small that she had to stand on a raised plank to reach the wheel. After the cloth was spun it was dyed with dye made from "shoemake" (sumac) leaves, green walnuts, reeds, and copperas. One person cut and others sewed. The dresses for women were straight, like slips, and the garments of the small boys resembled night shirts. If desired, a bias fold of contrasting colour was placed at the waist line or at the bottom of dresses. The crudely made garments were starched with a solution of flour or meal and water which was strained and then boiled.

As a small child Della remembers hearing a peculiar knock on the door during the night, and a voice which replied to queries, "No one to hurt you, but keep that red flannel in your mouth. Have you plenty to eat? Don't worry; you'll be free." No one would ever tell, if they knew, to whom this voice belonged.

Just before the beginning of the Civil War a comet appeared which was so bright that the elder people amused themselves by sitting on the rail fence and throwing pins upon the ground where the reflection was cast. The children scrambled madly to see who could find the most of the pins.

During the early part of the war Mr. Ross fought with the Confederates, leaving his young son, Robert, in charge of his affairs. The young master was very fond of horses and his favorite horse - "Bill" -- was trained to do tricks. One of these was to lie down when tickled on his flanks. The Yankees visited the plantation and tried to take this horse. Robert, who loved him dearly, refused to dismount, and as they were about to shoot the horse beneath him, the slaves began to plead. They explained that the boy was kind to every one and devoted to animals, after which explanation, he was allowed to keep his horse.

The breastworks at Savannah required many laborers to complete their construction, and as the commanders desired to save the strength of their soldiers, slave labor was solicited. Two slaves from each nearby plantation were sent to work for a limited number of days. The round trip from the Ross plantation required seven days.
Nearly every man had a family and when they returned from these long trips they drove to the quarters and fell on their knees to receive the welcome caresses of their small children.

Recreational facilities were not provided and slave children had little knowledge of how to play. Their two main amusements were building frog houses and sliding down a steep bank on a long board. One day, as they played up and down the highway, building frog houses at irregular intervals, little Della looked up and saw a group of Yankee calvarymen approaching. She screamed and began running and so attracted the attention of Mr. Ross who was at home on a furlough.
He saw the men in time to find a hiding place. Meanwhile, the soldiers arrived and the leader, springing from his horse, snatched Della up and spanked her soundly for giving the alarm, as they had hoped to take her master by surprise. Della said this was the first "white slap" she ever received.
Some of the Yankees entered the house, tore up the interior, and

threw the furniture out doors. Another group robbed the smokehouse and smashed so many barrels of syrup that it ran in a stream through the yard. They carried much of the meat off with them and gave the remainder to the slaves. Chickens were caught, dressed, and fried on the spot as each soldier carried his own frying pan, and a piece of flint rock and a sponge with which to make a fire. The men were skilled in dressing fowls and cleaned them in a few strokes.
When they had eaten as much as they desired, a search for the corral was made, but the mules were so well hidden that they were not able to find them. Della's father's hands were tied behind him and he was then forced to show them the hiding place. These fine beasts, used for plowing, were named by the slaves who worked them. Characteristic names were: "Jule", "Pigeon", "Little Deal", "Vic", (the carriage horse), "Streaked leg," "Kicking Kid", "Sore-back Janie". Every one was carried off.

This raid took place on Christmas Eve and the slaves were frantic as they had been told that Yankees were mean people, especially was Sherman so pictured.
When Sherman had gone, Mr. Ross came from his hiding place in the "cool well" and spoke to his slaves. To the elder ones he said, "I saw you give away my meat and mules."
"Master, we were afraid. We didn't want to do it, but we were afraid not to."
"Yes, I understand that you could not help yourselves." He then turnd to the children, saying, "Bless all of you, but to little Della, I owe my life. From now on she shall never be whipped, and she shall have a home of her own for life."
She shook with laughter as she said, "Master thought I screamed to

warn him and I was only frightened."

True to his word, after freedom he gave her a three-acre plot of land upon which he built a house and added a mule, buggy, cow, hogs, etc. Della lived there until after her marriage, when she had to leave with her husband. She later lost her home. Having been married twice, she now bears the name of Briscoe, her last husband's name.

When the family had again settled down to the ordinary routine, a new plague, body lice, said to have been left by the invaders, made life almost unbearable for both races.

Della now lives with her granddaughter, for she has been unable to work for twenty-eight years. Macon's Department of Public Welfare assists in contributing to her livelihood, as the granddaughter can only pay the room rent.

She does not know her age but believes that she is above ninety. Her keen old eyes seemed to look back into those bygone days as she said, "I got along better den dan I ever had since. We didn't know nuthin 'bout jail houses, paying for our burial grounds, and de rent. We had plenty o' food."

Dist. 6

Ex. Slv. - # 11

GEORGE BROOKS, EX-SLAVE.

Date of birth: Year unknown (See below).

Place of birth: In Muscogee County, near Columbus, Georgia.

Present residence: 502 - East 8th Street, Columbus, Georgia.

Interviewed: August 4, 1936.

This old darky, probably the oldest ex-slave in West Georgia, claims to be 112 years of age. His colored friends are also of the opinion that he is fully that old or older - - but, since none of his former (two) owners' people can be located, and no records concerning his birth can be found, his definite age cannot be positively established.

"Uncle" George claims to have worked in the fields, "some", the year the "stars fell" - - 1833.

His original owner was Mr. Beary Williams--to whom he was greatly attached. As a young man, he was--for a number of years--Mr. Williams' personal body-servant. After Mr. Williams' death--during the 1850's, "Uncle" George was sold to a white man--whose name he doesn't remember--of Dadeville, Alabama, with whom he subsequently spent five months in the Confederate service.

One of "Uncle" George's stories is to the effect that he once left a chore he was doing for his second "Marster's" wife, "stepped" to a nearby well to get a drink of water and, impelled by some strange, irresistible "power", "jes kep on walkin 'til he run slap-dab inter de Yankees", who corraled him and kept him for three months.

Still another story he tells is that of his being sold after freedom! According to his version of this incident, he was sold along with two bales of cotton in the fall of 1865--either the cotton being sold and he "thrown in" with it, or vice versa--he doesn't know which, but he does know that he and the cotton were "sold" together! And very soon after this transaction occurred, the seller was clapped in jail! Then, "somebody" (he doesn't remember who) gave him some money, put him on a stage-coach at night and "shipped" him to Columbus, where he learned that he was a free man and has since remained.

"Uncle" George has been married once and is the father of several children. His wife, however, died fifty-odd years ago and he knows nothing of the whereabouts of his children--doesn't even know whether or not any of them are living, having lost "all track o'all kin fokes too long ago to tawk about."

Unfortunately, "Uncle" George's mind is clouded and his memory badly impaired, otherwise his life story would perhaps be quite interesting. For more than twenty years, he has been supported and cared for by kind hearted members of his race, who say that they intend to continue "to look after the old man 'til he passes on."

100096

135

carded

(5) WR.

EX-SLAVE INTERVIEW

Easter Brown
1020 S. Lumpkin Street
Athens, Georgia

Written By: Mrs. Sadie B. Hornsby

and

Edited By: John N. Booth
Federal Writers' Project
WPA Residency No. 7

EASTER BROWN

"Aunt" Easter Brown, 78 years old, was sweeping chips into a basket out in front of her cabin. "Go right in honey, I'se comin' soon as I git some chips for my fire. Does I lak to talk 'bout when I wuz a chile? I sho does. I warn't but 4 years old when de war wuz over, but I knows all 'bout it."

"I wuz born in Floyd County sometime in October. My pa wuz Erwin and my ma wuz Liza Lorie. I don't know whar dey come from, but I knows dey wuz from way down de country somewhars. Dere wuz six of us chilluns. All of us wuz sold. Yessum, I wuz sold too. My oldest brother wuz named Jim. I don't riccolec' de others, dey wuz all sold off to diffunt parts of de country, and us never heared from 'em no more. My brother, my pa and me wuz sold on de block in Rome, Georgia. Marster Frank Glenn buyed me. I wuz so little dat when dey bid me off, dey had to hold me up so folkses could see me. I don't 'member my real ma and pa, and I called Marster 'pa' an' Mist'ess 'ma', 'til I wuz 'bout 'leven years old.

I don't know much 'bout slave quarters, or what dey had in 'em, 'cause I wuz raised in de house wid de white folkses. I does know beds in de quarters wuz lak shelves. Holes wuz bored in de side of de house, two in de wall and de floor, and poles runnin' from de wall and de floor, fastened together wid pegs; on 'em dey put planks, and cross de foot of de bed dey put a plank to hold de straw and keep de little 'uns from fallin' out.

"What did us have to eat? Lordy mussy! Mist'ess! us had everything. Summertime dere wuz beans, cabbage, squashes, irish 'tatoes, roas'en ears, 'matoes, cucumbers, cornbread, and fat meat, but de Nigger boys, dey wuz plum fools 'bout hog head. In winter dey et sweet 'tatoes, collards, turnips and sich, but I et lak de white folkses. I sho does lak 'possums and rabbits. Yessum, some of de slaves had gyardens, some of 'em sholy did.

"No'm, us Niggers never wore no clothes in summer, I means us little 'uns. In de winter us wore cotton clothes, but us went barefoots. My uncle Sam and some of de other Niggers went 'bout wid dey foots popped open from de cold. Marster had 110 slaves on his plantation.

"Mist'ess wuz good to me. Pa begged her to buy me, 'cause she wuz his young Mist'ess and he knowed she would be good to me, but Marster wuz real cruel. He'd beat his hoss down on his knees and he kilt one of 'em. He whupped de Niggers when dey didn't do right. Niggers is lak dis; dey wuz brought to dis here land wild as bucks, and dey is lak chicken roosters in a pen. You just have to make 'em 'have deyselves. Its lak dat now; if dey'd 'have dey-selves, white folkses would let 'em be.

"Dere warn't no jails in dem days. Dey had a gyuard house what dey whupped 'em in, and Mondays and Tuesdays wuz set aside for de whuppin's, when de Niggers what had done wrong got so many lash-es, 'cordin' to what devilment dey had been doin'. De overseer did-n't do de whuppin', Marster done dat. Dem patterrollers wuz sompin else. Mankind! If dey ketched a Nigger out atter dark widout no pass dey'd most nigh tear de hide offen his back.

"I'll tell you what dat overseer done one night. Some enemy of Marster's sot fire to de big frame house whar him and Mist'ess and de chillun lived. De overseer seed it burnin', and run and clam up de tree what wuz close to de house, went in de window and got Marster's two little gals out dat burnin' house 'fore you could say scat. Dat sho fixed de overseer wid old Marster. Atter dat Marster give him a nice house to live in but Marster's fine old house sho wuz burnt to de ground.

"De cyarriage driver wuz uncle Sam. He drove de chillun to school, tuk Marster and Mist'ess to church, and done de wuk 'round de house; such as, totin' in wood, keepin' de yards and waitin' on de cook. No'm us slaves didn't go to church; de Niggers wuz so wore out on Sundays, dey wuz glad to stay home and rest up, 'cause de overseer had 'em up way 'fore day and wuked 'em 'til long atter dark. On Saddays dey had to wash deir clothes and git ready for de next week. Some slaves might a had special things give to 'em on Christmas and New Years Day, but not on Marster's plantation; dey rested up a day and dat wuz all. I heared tell dey had Christmas fixin's and doin's on other plantations, but not on Marse Frank's place. All corn shuckin's, cotton pickin's, log rollin's, and de lak wuz when de boss made 'em do it, an' den dere sho warn't no extra sompin t'eat.

"De onliest game I ever played wuz to take my doll made out of a stick wid a rag on it and play under a tree. When I wuz big 'nough to wuk, all I done wuz to help de cook in de kitchen and play wid old Mist'ess' baby.

"Some of de Niggers runned away. Webster, Hagar, Atney, an' Jane runned away a little while 'fore freedom. Old Marster didn't try to git 'em back, 'cause 'bout dat time de war wuz over. Marster and Mist'ess sho looked atter de Niggers when dey got sick for dey knowed dat if a Nigger died dat much property wuz lost. Yessum, dey had a doctor sometime, but de most dey done wuz give 'em hoarhound, yellow root, and tansy. When a baby wuz cuttin' teeth, dey biled ground ivy and give 'em.

"Louisa, de cook wuz married in de front yard. All I 'members 'bout it wuz dat all de Niggers gathered in de yard, Louisa had on a white dress; de white folkses sho fixed Louisa up, 'cause she wuz deir cook.

"Jus' lemme tell you 'bout my weddin' I buyed myself a dress and had it laid out on de bed, den some triflin', no 'count Nigger wench tuk and stole it 'fore I had a chance to git married in it. I had done buyed dat dress for two pupposes; fust to git married in it, and second to be buried in. I stayed on wid Old Miss 'til I got 'bout grown and den I drifted to Athens. When I married my fust husband, Charlie Montgomery, I wuz wukkin' for Mrs. W. R. Booth, and us married in her dinin' room. Charlie died out and I married James Hoshier. Us had one baby. Hit wuz a boy. James an' our boy is both daid now and I'se all by myself.

"What de slaves done when dey wuz told dat dey wuz free? I wuz too little to know what dey meant by freedom, but Old Marster called de overseer and told him to ring de bell for de Niggers to come to de big house, He told 'em dey wuz free devils and dey could go whar dey pleased and do what dey pleased- dey could stay wid him if dey wanted to. Some stayed wid Old Marster and some went away. I never seed no yankee sojers. I heared tell of 'em comin' but I never seed none of 'em.

"No'm I don't know nothin' 'bout Abraham Lincoln, Booker T. Washington or Jefferson Davis. I didn't try to ketch on to any of 'em. As for slavery days; some of de Niggers ought to be free and some oughtn't to be. I don't know nuttin much 'bout it. I had a good time den, and I gits on pretty good now.

"How come I jined de church? Well I felt lak it wuz time for me to live better and git ready for a home in de next world. Chile you sho has axed me a pile of questions, and I has sho 'joyed tellin' you what I knowed."

****

Julia Brown (Aunt Sally)

710 Griffin Place, N. W.

Atlanta, Ga.

July 25, 1939

by

Geneva Tonsill

AH ALWAYS HAD A HARD TIME

Aunt Sally rocked back and forth incessantly. She mopped her wrinkled face with a dirty rag as she talked. "Ah wuz born fo' miles frum Commerce, Georgia, and wuz thirteen year ole at surrender. Ah belonged to the Nash fambly - three ole maid sisters. My mama belonged to the Nashes and my papa belonged to General Burns; he wuz a officer in the war. There wuz six of us chilluns, Lucy, Melvina, Johnnie,Callie, Joe and me. We didn't stay together long,as we wuz give out to different people. The Nashes didn't believe in selling slaves but we wuz known as their niggers. They sold one once 'cause the other slaves said they would kill him 'cause he had a baby by his own daughter. So to keep him frum bein' kilt, they sold him.

"My mama died the year of surrender. Ah didn't fare well after her death,Ah had sicha hard time. Ah wuz give to the Mitchell fambly and they done every cruel thing they could to me. Ah slept on the flo' nine years, winter and summer, sick or well. Ah never wore anything but a cotton dress, a shimmy and draw's. That 'oman didn't care what happened to the niggers. Sometime she would take us to church. We'd walk to the church house. Ah never went nowhere else. That 'oman took delight in sellin' slaves. She'd lash us with a cowhide whip. Ah had to shift fur mahself.

"They didn't mind the slaves matin', but they wanted their niggers to marry only amongst them on their place. They didn't 'low 'em to mate with other slaves frum other places. When the wimmen had babies they wuz treated kind and they let 'em stay in. We called it 'lay-in', just about lak they do now. We didn't go to no horspitals as they do now. We jest had our babies and had a granny to catch 'em. We didn't have all the pain-easin' medicines then. The granny would put a rusty piece of tin or a ax under the mattress and this would ease the pains. The granny put a ax under my mattress once. This wuz to cut off the after-pains and it sho did too, honey. We'd set up the fifth day and after the 'layin-in' time wuz up we wuz 'lowed to walk out doors and they tole us to walk around the house jest once and come in the house. This wuz to keep us frum takin' a 'lapse.

"We wuzn't 'lowed to go around and have pleasure as the folks does today. We had to have passes to go wherever we wanted. When we'd git out there wuz a bunch of white men called the 'patty rollers'. They'd come in and see if all us had passes and if they found any who didn't have a pass he wuz whipped; give fifty or more lashes--and they'd count them lashes. If they said a hundred you got a hundred. They wuz somethin' lak the Klu Klux. We wuz 'fraid to tell our masters about the Patty Rollers because we wuz skeered they'd whip us again,fur we wuz tole not to tell. They'd sing a little ditty. Ah wish Ah could remember the words, but it went somethin' lak this;

'Run,Niggah,run, de Patty Rollers'll git you,
Run Niggah, run, you'd bettah git away.'

"We wuz 'fraid to go any place.

"Slaves were treated in most cases lak cattle. A man went about the country buyin' up slaves lak buyin' up cattle and the like, and he wuz called a 'speculator', then he'd sell 'em to the highest bidder. Oh! it wuz pitiful to see chil'en taken frum their mothers' breast, mothers sold, husbands sold frum wives. One 'oman he wuz to buy had a baby, and of course the baby come befo' he bought her and he wouldn't buy the baby; said he hadn't bargained to buy the baby too, and he jest wouldn't. My uncle wuz married but he wuz owned by one master and his wife wuz owned by another. He wuz 'lowed to visit his wife on Wednesday and Saturday, that's the onliest time he could git off.

He went on Wednesday and when he went back on Saturday his wife had been bought by the speculator and he never did know where she wuz.

"Ah worked hard always. Honey, you can't 'magine what a hard time Ah had. Ah split rails lak a man. How did Ah do it? Ah used a huge glut, and a iron wedge drove into the wood with a maul, and this would split the wood.

"Ah help spin the cotton into thread fur our clothes. The thread wuz made into big broaches -- four broaches made four cuts, or one hank. After the thread wuz made we used a loom to weave the cloth. We had no sewin' machine-- had to sew by hand. My mistress had a big silver bird and she would always catch the cloth in the bird's bill and this would hold it fur her to sew.

"Ah didn't git to handle money when I wuz young. Ah worked frum sunup to sundown. We never had overseers lak some of the slaves. We wuz give so much work to do in a day and if the white folks went off on a vacation they would give us so much work to do while they wuz gone and we better have all of that done too when they'd come home. Some of the white folks wuz very kind to their slaves. Some did not believe in slavery and some freed them befo' the war and even give 'em land and homes. Some would give the niggers meal, lard and lak that. They made me hoe when Ah wuz a chile and Ah'd keep rat up with the others, 'cause they'd tell me that if Ah got behind a run-a-way nigger would git me and split open my head and git the milk out'n it. Of course Ah didn't know then that wuzn't true -- Ah believed everything they tole me and that made me work the harder.

"There wuz a white man, Mister Jim, that wuz very mean to the slaves. He'd go 'round and beat 'em. He'd even go to the little homes, tear down the chimneys and do all sorts of cruel things. The chimneys wuz made of mud 'n straw 'n sticks; they wuz powerful strong too. Mister Jim wuz jest a mean man, and when he died we all said God got tired of Mister Jim being so mean and kilt him. When they laid him out on the coolin' board, everybody wuz settin' 'round, moanin' over his death, and all of a sudden Mister Jim rolled off'n the coolin' board, and sich a runnin' and gittin' out'n that room you never saw. We said Mister Jim wuz tryin' to run the niggers and we wuz 'freid to go about at night. Ah believed it then; now that they's 'mbalmin' Ah know that must have been gas and he wuz purgin', fur they didn't know nothin' 'bout 'mbalmin' then. They didn't keep dead folks out'n the ground long in them days.

"Doctors wuzn't so plentiful then. They'd go 'round in buggies and on hosses. Them that rode on a hoss had saddle pockets jest filled with little bottles and lots of them. He'd try one medicine and if it didn't do not good he'd try another until it did do good and when the doctor went to see a sick pusson he'd stay rat there until he wuz better. He didn't jest come in and write a 'scription fur somebody to take to a drug store. We used herbs a lots in them days. When a body had dropsy we'd set him in a tepid bath made of mullein leaves. There wuz a jimson weed we'd use fur rheumatism, and fur asthma we'd use tea made of chestnut leaves. We'd git the chestnut leaves, dry them in the sun jest lak tea leaves, and we wouldn't let them leaves git wet fur nothin' in the world while they wuz dryin'. We'd take poke salad roots, boil them and then take sugar and make a syrup. This wuz the best thing fur asthma. It wuz known to cure it too. Fur colds and sich we used ho'hound; made candy out'n it with brown sugar. We used a lots of rock candy and whiskey fur colds too. They had a remedy that they used fur consumption - take dry cow manure, make a tea of this and flavor it with mint and give it to the sick pusson. We didn't need many doctors then fur we didn't have so much sickness in them days, and nachelly they didn't die so fast; folks lived a long time then. They used a lot of peachtree leaves too for fever,and when the stomach got upsot we'd crush the leaves, pour water over them and wouldn't let them drink any other kind of water 'till they wuz better. Ah still believes in them ole ho'made medicines too and Ah don't believe in so many doctors.

"We didn't have stoves plentiful then; just ovens we set in the fireplace. Ah's toted a many a armful of bark — good ole hickory bark to cook with. We'd cook light bread - both flour and corn. The yeast fur this bread wuz made frum hops. Coals of fire wuz put on top of the oven and under the bottom, too. Everything wuz cooked on coals frum a wood fire - coffee and all. Wait, let me show you my coffee tribet. Have you ever seen one? Well, Ah'll show you mine." Aunt Sally got up and hobbled to the kitchen to get the trivet. After a few moments search she came back into the room.

"No, it's not there. Ah guess it's been put in the basement. Ah'll show it to you when you come back. It's a rack made of iron that the pot is set on befo' puttin' it on the fire coals. The victuals wuz good in them days; we got our vegetables out'n the garden in season and didn't have all the hot-house vegetables. Ah don't eat many vegetables now unless they come out'n the garden and I know it. Well, as I said, there wuz racks fitted in the fireplace to put pots on. Once there wuz a big pot settin' on the fire, jest bilin' away with a big roast in it. As the water biled, the meat turned over and over, comin' up to the top and goin' down again. Ole Sandy, the dog, come in the kitchen. He sot there a while and watched that meat roll over and over in the pot, and all of a sudden-like he grabbed at that meat and pulls it out'n the pot. 'Course he couldn't eat it 'cause it wuz hot and they got the meat befo' he et it. The kitchen wuz away frum the big house, so the victuals wuz cooked and carried up to the house. Ah'd carry it up mahse'f. We couldn't eat all the different kinds of victuals the white folks et and one mornin' when I wuz carryin' the breakfast to the big house we had waffles that wuz a pretty golden brown and pipin' hot. They wuz a picture to look at and Ah jest couldn't keep frum takin' one, and that wuz the hardest waffle fur me to eat befo' I got to the big house I ever saw. Ah jest couldn't git rid of that waffle 'cause my conscience whipped me so.

"They taught me to do everything. Ah'd use battlin' blocks and battlin' sticks to wash the clothes; we all did. The clothes wuz taken out of the water on put on the block and beat with a battlin' stick, which was made like a paddle. On wash days you could hear them battlin' sticks poundin' every which-away. We made our own soap, used ole meat and grease, and poured water over wood ashes which wuz kept in a rack-like thing and the water would drip through the ashes. This made strong lye. We used a lot 'o sich lye, too, to bile with.

"Sometimes the slaves would run away. Their masters wuz mean to them that caused them to run away. Sometimes they would live in caves. How did they get along? Well, chile, they got along all right—what with other people slippin' things in to 'em. And, too, they'd steal hogs, chickens, and anything else they could git their hands on. Some white people would help, too, fur there wuz some white people who didn't believe in slavery. Yes, they'd try to find them slaves that run away and if they wuz found they'd be beat or sold to somebody else. My grandmother run away frum her master. She stayed in the woods and she washed her clothes in the branches. She used sand fur soap. Yes, chile, I reckon they got 'long all right in the caves. They had babies in thar and raised 'em, too.

"Ah stayed with the Mitchells 'til Miss Hannah died. Ah even helped to lay her out. Ah didn't go to the graveyard though. Ah didn't have a home after she died and Ah wandered frum place to place, stayin' with a white fambly this time and then a nigger fambly the next time. Ah moved to Jackson County and stayed with a Mister Frank Dowdy. Ah didn't stay there long though. Then Ah moved to Winder, Georgia. They called it 'Jug Tavern' in them days, 'cause jugs wuz made there. Ah married Green Hinton in Winder. Got along well after marryin' him. He farmed fur a livin' and made a good livin' fur me and the eight chilluns, all born in Winder. The chilluns wuz grown nearly when he died and wuz able to help me with the smalles ones. Ah got along all right after his death and didn't have sich a hard time raisin' the chilluns. Then Ah married Jim Brown and moved to Atlanta. Jim farmed at first fur a livin' and then he worked on the railroad — the Seaboard. He helped to grade the first railroad track for that line. He wuz a sand-dryer."

Aunt Sally broke off her story here. "Lord, honey, Ah got sich a pain in mah stomach Ah don't believe Ah can go on. It's a gnawin' kind 'o pain. Jest keeps me weak all over." Naturally I suggested that we complete the story at another time. So I left, promisin' to return in a few days. A block from the house I stopped in a store to order some groceries fur Aunt Sally. The proprietress, a Jewish woman, spoke up when I gave the delivery address. She explained in broken English that she knew Aunt Sally.

"I tink you vas very kind to do dis for Aunt Sally. She neets it. I often gif her som food. He's very old and feeble. He passed here yesterday and he look so wasted and hungry. His stomick look like it vas drawn in, you know. I gif him some fresh hocks. I know dey could not eat all of them in a day and I'm afrait it von't be goof for dem today. I vas trained to help people in neet. It's part of my religion. See, if ve sit on de stritcar and an olt person comes in and finds no seat, ve get up and gif him one. If ve see a person loaded vid bundles and he iss old and barely able to go, ve gif a hand. See, ve Jews — you colored — but ve know no difference. Anyvon neeting help, ve gif."

A couple of days later I was back at Aunt Sally's. I had brought some groceries for the old woman. I knocked a long time on the front door, and, getting no answer, I picked my way through the rank growth of weeds and grass surrounding the house and went around to the back door. It opened into the kitchen, where Aunt Sally and her son were having breakfast. The room was small and dark and I could hardly see the couple, but Aunt Sally welcomed me. Lawd, honey, you come right on in. I tole John I heard somebody knockin' at the do'."

"You been hearin' things all mornin'," John spoke up. He turned to me. "You must've been thinkin' about mamma just when we started eatin' breakfast because she asked me did I hear somebody call her. I tole her the Lawd Jesus is always a-callin' poor niggers, but she said it sounded like the lady's voice who was here the other day. Well I didn't hear anything and I tole her she mus' be hearin' things."

I'd put the bag of groceries on the table unobtrusively, but Aunt Sally wasn't one to let such gifts pass unnoticed. Eagerly she tore the bag open and began pulling out the packages. "Lawd bless you, chile, and He sho will bless you! I feels rich seein' what you brought me. Jest look at this --- Lawdy mercy! --- rolls, butter, milk, balogny...! Oh, this balogny, jest looky there! You must a knowed what I wanted!" She was stuffing it in her mouth as she talked. "And these aigs...! Honey, you knows God is goin' to bless you and let you live long. Ah'se goin' to cook one at a time. And Ah sho been wantin' some milk. Ah'se gonna cook me a hoecake rat now."

She went about putting the things in little cans and placing them on shelves or in the dilapidated little cupboard that stood in a corner. I sat down near the door and listened while she rambled on.

"Ah used to say young people didn't care bout ole folks but Ah is takin' that back now. Ah jest tole my son the other day that its turned round, the young folks thinks of the ole and tries to help 'em and the ole folks don't try to think of each other; some of them, they is too mean. Ah can't understand it; Ah jest know I heard you call me when Ah started to eat, and tole my son so. Had you been to the do' befo'?" She talked on not waiting for a reply. "Ah sho did enjoy the victuals you sent day befo' yistidy. They send me surplus food frum the gove'mment but Ah don't like what they send. The skim milk gripes me and Ah don't like that yellow meal. A friend brought me some white meal t'other day. And that wheat cereal they send! Ah eats it with water when Ah don't have milk and Ah don't like it but when you don't have nothin' else you got to eat what you have. They send me 75¢ ever two weeks but that don't go very fur. Ah ain't complainin' fur Ah'm thankful fur what Ah git.

"They send a girl to help me around the house, too. She's frum the housekeepin' department. She's very nice to me. Yes, she sho'ly is a sweet girl, and her foreman is sweet too. She comes in now 'n then to see me and see how the girl is gittin' along. She washes, too. Ah's been on relief a long time. Now when Ah first got on it wuz when they first started givin' me. They give me plenty of anything Ah asked fur and my visitor wuz Mrs. Tompkins. She wuz so good to me. Well they stopped that and then the DPW (Department of Public Welfare) took care of me. When they first started Ah got more than I do now and they've cut me down 'till Ah gits only a mighty little.

"Yes, Ah wuz talkin' about my husband when you wuz here t'other day. He wuz killed on the railroad. After he moved here he bought this home. Ah'se lived here twenty years. Jim wuz comin' in the railroad yard one day and stepped off the little engine they used for the workers rat in the path of the L.& N. train. He wuz cut up and crushed to pieces. He didn't have a sign of a head. They used a rake to git up the pieces they did git. A man brought a few pieces out here in a bundle and Ah wouldn't even look at them.

Ah got a little money frum the railroad but the lawyer got most of it. He brought me a few dollars out and tole me not to discuss it with anyone nor tell how much Ah got. Ah tried to git some of the men that worked with him to tell me just how it all happened, but they wouldn't talk, and it wuz scand'lous how them niggers held their peace and wouldn't tell me anything. The boss man came out later but he didn't seem intrusted in it at all, so Ah got little or nothing fur his death. The lawyer got it fur hisse'f.

"All my chilluns died 'cept my son and he is ole and sick and can't do nothin' fur me or hisse'f. He gets relief too, 75¢ every two weeks. He goes 'round and people gives him a little t'eat. He has a hard time tryin' to git 'long.

"Ah had a double bed in t'other room and let a woman have it so she could git some of the delegates to the Baptist World Alliance and she wuz goin' to pay me fur lettin' her use the bed, but she didn't git anybody 'cept two. They come there on Friday and left the next day. She wuz tole that they didn't act right 'bout the delegates and lots of people went to the expense to prepare fur them and didn't git a one. Ah wuz sorry, fur Ah intended to use what she paid me fur my water bill. Ah owes $3.80 and had to give my deeds to my house to a lady to pay the water bill fur me and it worries me 'cause Ah ain't got no money to pay it, fur this is all Ah got and Ah hates to loose my house. Ah wisht it wuz some way to pay it. Ah ain't been able to do fur mahse'f in many years now, and has to depend on what others gives me.

"Tell you mo' about the ole times? Lawd, honey, times has changed so frum when Ah was young. You don't hear of haints as you did when I growed up. The Lawd had to show His work in miracles 'cause we didn't have learnin' in them days as they has now. And you may not believe it but them things happened. Ah knows a old man what died, and after his death he would come to our house where he always cut wood, and at night we could hear a chain bein' drug along in the yard, jest as if a big log-chain wuz bein' pulled by somebody. It would drag on up to the woodpile and stop, then we could hear the thump-thump of the ax on the wood. The woodpile was near the chimney and it would chop-chop on, then stop and we could hear the chain bein' drug back the way it come. This went on fur several nights until my father got tired and one night after he head it so long, the chop-chop, papa got mad and hollered at the haint, 'G-- D... you, go to hell!!!' and that spirit went off and never did come back!

"We'd always know somebody wuz goin' to die when we heard a owl come to a house and start screechin'. We always said, 'somebody is gwine to die!' Honey, you don't hear it now and it's good you don't fur it would skeer you to death nearly. It sounded so mo'nful like and we'd put the poker or the shovel in the fire and that always run him away; it burned his tongue out and he couldn't holler no more. If they'd let us go out lak we always wanted to, Ah don't 'spects we'd a-done it, 'cause we wuz too skeered. Lawdy, chile, them wuz tryin' days. Ah sho is glad God let me live to see these 'uns.

"Ah tried to git the ole-age pension fur Ah sho'ly needed it and wuz 'titled to it too. Sho wuz. But that visitor jest wouldn't let me go through. She acted lak that money belonged to her. Ah 'plied when it first come out and shoulda been one of the first to get one. Ah worried powerful much at first fur Ah felt how much better off Ah'd be. Ah wouldn't be so dependent lak Ah'm is now. Ah 'spects you knows that 'oman. She is a big black 'oman -- wuz named Smith at first befo' she married. She is a Johns now. She sho is a mean 'oman. She jest wouldn't do no way. Ah even tole her if she let me go through and Ah got my pension Ah would give her some of the money Ah got, but she jest didn't do no way. She tole me if Ah wuz put on Ah'd get no more than Ah <u>wuz</u> gittin'. Ah sho believes them thats on gits more'n 75¢ every two weeks. Ah sho had a hard time and a roughety road to travel with her my visitor until they sent in the housekeeper. Fur that head 'oman jest want rat out and got me some clothes. Everything Ah needed. When Ah tole her how my visitor wuz doin' me she jest went out and come rat back with all the things Ah needed. Ah don't know why my visitor done me lak that. Ah said at first it wuz because Ah had this house but honey, what could Ah do with a house when Ah wuz hongry and not able to work. Ah always worked hard. 'Course Ah didn't git much fur it but Ah lak to work fur what Ah gits."

Aunt Sally was beginning to repeat herself and I began to suspect she was talking just to please me. So I arose to go.

"Lawsy mercy, chile, you sho is sweet to set here and talk to a ole 'oman lak me. Ah sho is glad you come. Ah tole my son you wuz a bundle of sunshine and Ah felt so much better the day you left - and heah you is again! Chile, my nose wuzn't itchin' fur nothin'! You come back to see me real soon. Ah'se always glad to have you. And the Lawd's gonna sho go with you fur bein' so good to me."

My awareness of the obvious fulsomeness in the old woman's praise in no way detracted from my feeling of having done a good deed. Aunt Sally was a clever psychologist and as I carefully picked my way up the weedy path toward the street, I felt indeed that the "Lawd" was "sho goin'" with me.

EX-SLAVE INTERVIEW

JULIA BUNCH
Beech Island
South Carolina

Written by: Leila Harris
Augusta -

Edited by: John N. Booth
District Supervisor
Federal Writers' Project
Res. 6 & 7

JULIA BUNCH
Ex-Slave - Age 85

Seated in a comfortable chair in the living room of her home, Julia Bunch, Negress of 85 years, presented a picture of the old South that will soon pass away forever. The little 3-room house, approachable only on foot, was situated on top of a hill. Around the clean-swept yard, petunias, verbena, and other flowers were supplemented by a large patch of old-fashioned ribbon grass. A little black and white kitten was frisking about and a big red hen lazily scratched under a big shade tree in search of food for her brood. Julia's daughter, who was washing "white people's clothes" around the side of the house, invited us into the living room where her mother was seated.

The floors of the front porch and the living room were scrubbed spotlessly clean. There was a rug on the floor, while a piano across one corner, a chifforobe with mirrored doors, a bureau, and several comfortable chairs completed the room's furnishings. A motley assortment of pictures adorning the walls included: The Virgin Mother, The Sacred Bleeding Heart, several large family photographs, two pictures of the Dionne Quintuplets, and one of President Roosevelt.

Julia was not very talkative, but had a shy, irresistible chuckle, and it was this, together with her personal appearance and the tidiness of her home that left an indelible impression on the minds of her visitors. Her skin was very dark, and her head closely wrapped in a dark bandana, from which the gray hair peeped at intervals forming a frame for her face. She was clad in a black and white flowered print dress and a dark gray sweater, from which a white ruffle was apparent at the neck. Only two buttons of the sweater were fastened and it fell away at the waist displaying her green striped apron. From beneath the long dress, her feet were visible encased in men's black shoes laced with white strings. Her ornaments consisted of a ring on her third finger, earrings, and tortoise-rimmed glasses which plainly displayed their dime-store origin.

"I b'longed to Marse Jackie Dorn of Edgefield County, I was gived to him and his wife when dey was married for a weddin' gift. I nussed deir three chilluns for 'em and slep' on a couch in dier bedroom 'til I was 12 years old, den 'Mancipation come. I loved 'em so and stayed wid 'em for four years atter freedom and when I left 'em I cried and dem chilluns cried.

"Yassir, dey was sho' good white people and very rich. Dere warn't nothin' lackin' on dat plantation. De big house was part wood and part brick, and de Niggers lived in one or two room box houses built in rows. Marse Jackie runned a big grist mill and done de grindin' for all de neighbors 'round 'bout. Three or four Niggers wukked in de mill all de time. Us runned a big farm and dairy too.

"Dere was allus plenty t'eat 'cause Marster had a 2-acre gyarden and a big fruit orchard. Two cooks was in de kitchen all de time. Dey cooked in a big fireplace, but us had big ovens to cook de meat, biscuits and lightbread in. Us made 'lasses and syrup and put up fruits just lak dey does now.

"My Ma was head weaver. It tuk two or three days to set up de loom 'cause dere was so many little bitty threads to be threaded up. Us had dyes of evvy color. Yassir, us could make wool cloth too. De sheeps was sheered once a year and de wool was manufactured up and us had a loom wid wheels to spin it into thread.

"Old Marster never whupped nobody and dere was only one man dat I kin 'member dat de overseer whupped much and he 'served it 'cause he would run away in spite of evvything. Dey would tie him to a tree way down in de orchard and whup him."

Julia kept repeating and seemed anxious to impress upon the minds of her visitors that her white folks were good and very rich. "Yassir, my white folks had lots of company and visited a lot. Dey rode saddle horses and had deir own carriages wid a high seat for de driver. Nosir, she didn't ride wid hoopskirts - you couldn't ride wid dem on.

"Us bought some shoes from de market but dere was a travelin' shoemaker dat wukked by days for all de folks. He was a slave and didn't git no money; it was paid to his Marster. Us had our own blacksmith dat wukked all de time.

"De slaves from all de plantations 'round come to our corn shuckin's. Us had 'em down in de orchard. Lots of white folks comed too. Dey kilt hogs and us had a big supper and den us danced. Nosir, dere warn't no toddy, Marse didn't b'lieve in dat, but dey would beat up apples and us drinked de juice. It sho' was sweet too.

"Folks done dey travelin' in stages and hacks in dem days. Each of de stages had four hosses to 'em. When de cotton and all de other things was ready to go to market, dey would pack 'em and bring 'em to Augusta wid mules and wagons. It would take a week and sometimes longer for de trip, and dey would come back loaded down wid 'visions and clothes, and dere was allus a plenty for all de Niggers too.

"De white folks allus helped deir Niggers wid de weddin's and buyed deir clothes for 'em. I 'members once a man friend of mine come to ax could he marry one of our gals. Marster axed him a right smart of questions and den he told him he could have her, but he mustn't knock or cuff her 'bout when he didn't want her no more, but to turn her loose.

"Us had a big cemetery on our place and de white folks allus let deir Niggers come to de fun'rals. De white folks had deir own sep'rate buryin' ground, but all de coffins was home-made. Even de ones for de settlement peoples was made right in our shop. Yassum, dey sung at de fun'rals and you wants me to sing. I can't sing, but I'll try a little bit." Then with a beautiful and peculiar rhythm only attained by the southern Negro, she chanted:

'Come-ye-dat-love-de-Lord
And-let-your-joys-be-known.'

"A rooster crowin' outside your door means company's comin' and a squinch owl means sho' death. Dose are all de signs I kin 'member and I don't 'member nothin' 'bout slavery remedies.

"Yassir, dey useter give us a nickle or 10 cents sometimes so us could buy candy from de store." Asked if she remembered patterollers she gave her sly chuckle and said: "I sho' does. One time dey come to our house to hunt for some strange Niggers. Dey didn't find 'em but I was so skeered I hid de whole time dey was dar. Yassir, de Ku Kluxers raised cain 'round dar too.

"I 'members de day well when Marster told us us was free.

I was glad and didn't know what I was glad 'bout. Den 'bout 200 Yankee soldiers come and dey played music right dar by de roadside. Dat was de fust drum and fife music I ever heared. Lots of de Niggers followed 'em on off wid just what dey had on. None of our Niggers went and lots of 'em stayed right on atter freedom.

"Four years atter dat, I left Edgefield and come here wid my old man. Us had six chilluns. My old man died six years ago right dar 'cross de road and I'se livin' here wid my daughter. I can't wuk no more, I tried to hoe a little out dar in de field last year and I fell down and I hasn't tried no more since.

"I went once not so long ago to see my white folkses. Dey gived me a dollar to spend for myself and I went 'cross de street and buyed me some snuff - de fust I had had for a long time. Dey wanted to know if I had ever got de old age pension and said dat if I had been close to dem I would have had it 'fore now."

TITLES IN THE

SLAVE NARRATIVES SERIES

FROM APPLEWOOD BOOKS

ALABAMA SLAVE NARRATIVES
ISBN 1-55709-010-6 • $14.95
Paperback • 7-1/2" x 9-1/4" • 168 pp

ARKANSAS SLAVE NARRATIVES
ISBN 1-55709-011-4 • $14.95
Paperback • 7-1/2" x 9-1/4" • 172 pp

FLORIDA SLAVE NARRATIVES
ISBN 1-55709-012-2 • $14.95
Paperback • 7-1/2" x 9-1/4" • 168 pp

GEORGIA SLAVE NARRATIVES
ISBN 1-55709-013-0 • $14.95
Paperback • 7-1/2" x 9-1/4" • 172 pp

INDIANA SLAVE NARRATIVES
ISBN 1-55709-014-9 • $14.95
Paperback • 7-1/2" x 9-1/4" • 140 pp

KENTUCKY SLAVE NARRATIVES
ISBN 1-55709-016-5 • $14.95
Paperback • 7-1/2" x 9-1/4" • 136 pp

MARYLAND SLAVE NARRATIVES
ISBN 1-55709-017-3 • $14.95
Paperback • 7-1/2" x 9-1/4" • 88 pp

MISSISSIPPI SLAVE NARRATIVES
ISBN 1-55709-018-1 • $14.95
Paperback • 7-1/2" x 9-1/4" • 184 pp

MISSOURI SLAVE NARRATIVES
ISBN 1-55709-019-X • $14.95
Paperback • 7-1/2" x 9-1/4" • 172 pp

NORTH CAROLINA SLAVE NARRATIVES
ISBN 1-55709-020-3 • $14.95
Paperback • 7-1/2" x 9-1/4" • 168 pp

OHIO SLAVE NARRATIVES
ISBN 1-55709-021-1 • $14.95
Paperback • 7-1/2" x 9-1/4" • 128 pp

OKLAHOMA SLAVE NARRATIVES
ISBN 1-55709-022-X • $14.95
Paperback • 7-1/2" x 9-1/4" • 172 pp

SOUTH CAROLINA SLAVE NARRATIVES
1-55709-023-8 • $14.95
Paperback • 7-1/2" x 9-1/4" • 172 pp

TENNESSEE SLAVE NARRATIVES
ISBN 1-55709-024-6 • $14.95
Paperback • 7-1/2" x 9-1/4" • 92 pp

VIRGINIA SLAVE NARRATIVES
ISBN 1-55709-025-4 • $14.95
Paperback • 7-1/2" x 9-1/4" • 68 pp

* * * * * * * * * * * * * * * * * *

IN THEIR VOICES: SLAVE NARRATIVES
A companion CD of original recordings made by the Federal Writers' Project. Former slaves from many states tell stories, sing long-remembered songs, and recall the era of American slavery. This invaluable treasure trove of oral history, through the power of voices of those now gone, brings back to life the people who lived in slavery.
ISBN 1-55709-026-2 • $19.95
Audio CD

* * * * * * * * * * * * * * * * * *

TO ORDER, CALL 800-277-5312 OR
VISIT US ON THE WEB AT WWW.AWB.COM

CPSIA information can be obtained
at www.ICGtesting.com
Printed in the USA
JSHW041942250221
12060JS00005B/104

9 781557 090133